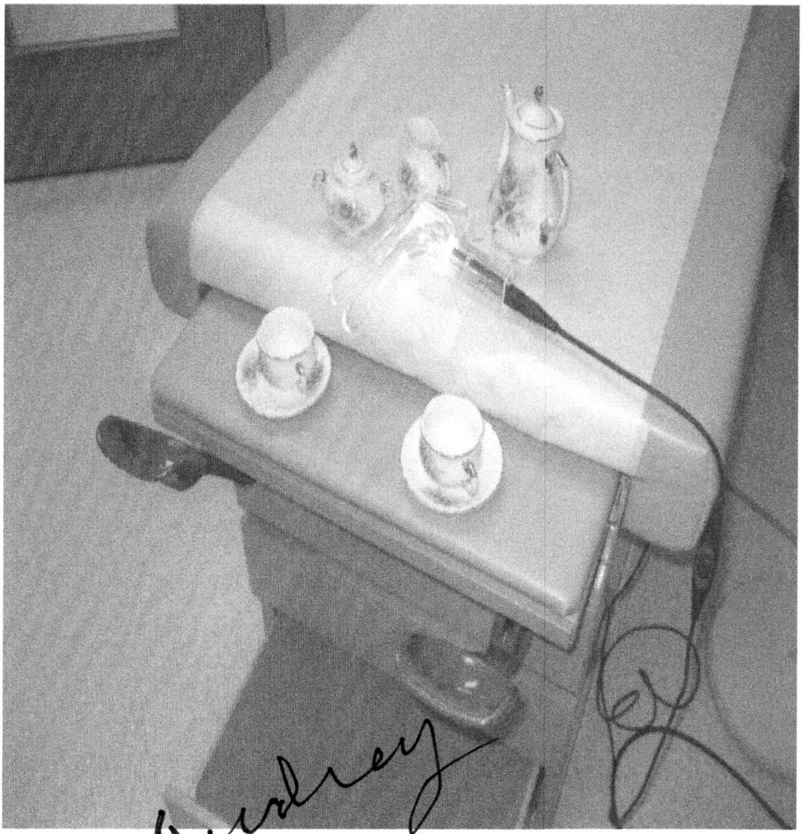

Mrs. A's Tea Party

Two Pregnant Teens. Three Options

A Novel

by Marj Helmer

ISBN: 979-8-9856443-9-5
Library of Congress Control Number:
2022907814
Cover by: Marj Helmer and Lise Spence-Parsons

Contents

DEDICATION

Thank you to you, the reader reading this story. I wrote it for you and for all who may decide to be a parent. Thank you to my friend Karen Anderson Rader and her mother Marion. Together they modeled my Mrs. A, in her kindness, caring and serving nature. Thank you to my "Writing Buddy," Gloria Olson, for the early years of support as we struggled to be "WRITERS." Gloria was a fantastic teacher and is a great writer. Thank you to "the Maple Grove Writers' Studio" which has brought me to publication with love, respect and writing support beyond measure. I love you all. And to my family, especially Don. I want to acknowledge their love and encouragement over the many years I took to create this story.

PROLOGUE

"Hi, Mrs. A," Cheryl called to the older woman coming down the hall.

The response was lost in the explosion. Cheryl and the receptionist disappeared in a bloody vapor and metal shower that flew out from between them. Their bodies thudded to the floor yards away from each other. Mrs. A was forced back down the hall and landed on her back with the metal and wood piercing her blooded body, face, and arms. Her own blood soon mixed with that already covering her. She could feel her leg folded weirdly to the side. Everything was muffled. She couldn't hear and with the blood in her eyes, she couldn't see. Someone ran past. Someone else was kneeling next to her. She could see that person yelling at her, but she couldn't hear or answer.

Marj Helmer

Chapter 1

There had been so many girls and women. Why did they keep coming? Tearing her apart with their pregnancies. She helped them and stood by them. They were around for a while and then got on with their lives. Mostly she lost track of them.

But things were changing. There weren't as many coming now. Roe v Wade had made a difference. More options were available, and women didn't have to be rich to have safe procedures and good care. Still, they came for help, like Cheryl, who had appeared before the tea party. Her pleas had been so simple.

"You helped so many, can't you help me?"

"Help you how, Cheryl?" Mrs. A said and waited.

"I can't go through with it! I can't face my friends! This is going to ruin everything! Crap!" She raced back and forth between the table and the door, her, young, fresh face flashing pain and terror. Haunted. Scared. Cheryl kept cursing. Her self-loathing causing the curses to come louder and more fiercely. Each time she got close to the door, Mrs. A thought she would yank it open and bolt. But what would she bolt to? Or, for that matter, from? The problem that brought her to the house today was within her. There was no escape, not now, not ever. Mrs. A knew that even when Cheryl's problem was "solved," that problem was flesh of her flesh and indivisible from her forever.

Then, as she reached the door again, Cheryl turned and crashed against it, sliding to the floor. With her collapse, the cursing was replaced with sobs that were so violent, she beat her temples in order to make them stop, hoping the pain would give her control again.

Still Mrs. A waited. Cheryl calmed herself enough to stop the hitting. She banged her head several times back against the door. She began to take deep breaths. She wiped her eyes with the backs of her hands and her nose with the sleeve of her shirt.

Cheryl wasn't a pretty girl. She was tall and broad shouldered with some heft to her. Strong. Athletic. Not ugly, but not pretty. The ravages of her emotion had made her eyes red and swollen. Her skin was also red and blotchy. Her hair had come mostly out of the tight ponytail she wore. The mess actually made her more feminine, more fragile, more attractive. It softened her. Made her more sympathetic. Or was it that it made her only, after all, look vulnerable.

Mrs. A shifted in her chair. Cheryl looked up through the mess of her pain and anger. "I know you'll help either way," she said. "I've heard the talk."

Mrs. A waited, her eyes connected to the pleading face of the young girl. What did she want from her? Why did they keep coming to her? How had this all begun? What difference did it make? The only thing that mattered now was this drama in her kitchen. This young life "ruined," if she were to believe the woman before her.

For woman she was. She had been doing womanly things and her body had betrayed her. Her plans, her dreams, her hopes. Yes, even as young as she was, they were there. Plans, dreams, hopes. Ill formed or unformed, they were there.

"You know, I gotta play. I can't let the team down. I'm so tired." Cheryl shifted her anxious eyes to the floor. "All I do is cry. I can't be around anyone, 'cause they'll know. They'll ask. They're already on me about not being around. I tell 'em I'm anemic...."

"You probably are," Mrs. A said. "Your body is meeting extra demands." But it wasn't time to speak yet. Cheryl was not listening.

"But they will know. And I can't have that. I can't lose. They'll hate me. I'm supposed to be the leader. They made me team captain! They look up to me. I can't do it! Can't do it! Oh God ...! Oh God." The last words were more like a moan than a prayer.

"And Kenny! He's such a kid. He has no idea. He is actually older, but he's such a kid. How could I ever...? Well, I did, obviously, or I wouldn't be here like this. Oh crap!" The anger was coming back, but she stopped it. She shook her head.

So much for Kenny. No help there. "Such a kid!" Mrs. A thought with a shake of her head, things like this made adults out of kids. But Kenny wasn't going to know. Wasn't going to grow with Cheryl. Wasn't going to suffer. She almost added "the consequences." But she didn't need to. Suffer was right. Cheryl would suffer. Kenny would not. She might even continue with him. Her choice. She certainly seemed concerned with how things looked. So, she might.

Cheryl was getting up. In a strong movement of her body, she reached her height, straightened her shoulders, grew a couple inches taller with resolution and came over to the table. Standing there, the fingers of her right hand lightly pressing the tabletop, she said quietly, "Please help me."

•* * * * * *

"Please help me."

Mrs. A said, "Sit down." Firmly. Not a command, not a request. And Cheryl sat. Now, she was ready to listen. She was exhausted, resigned, determined. Mrs. A got up, opened the fridge and took out a pitcher of cold water. She placed it on the table and walked to the cupboard. Getting two glasses, she came back to the table and sat down again. Her body was angled toward the girl who was sitting with her right hand resting on the formica. Cheryl slumped, her hips forward on the seat, her shoulders touching the back of the chair, and her head down toward her chest. She looked beaten. Waiting for judgment.

Mrs. A poured water into the glasses. She slid one over to Cheryl who reached for it without looking up.

"You could give it ...," Mrs. A started.

But Cheryl almost screamed. "No! I can't! I'll die!" There was a long silence. Cheryl sat there looking at the floor.

"So," Mrs. A said. "How long?"

"Prom. Isn't that stupid? Soooo romantic. Ha! What a dope! I shoulda.... Oh God." Anger to pain, the expressions ran across her face. The emotions slid into each other. She stomped her foot and slapped the table with her hand, and then her body sagged again.

"I ask only to figure out the possibilities. I won't always help with this. It depends on the timing." As if that made any difference, she thought.

Mrs. A got up again and walked to the counter. She opened a drawer, glancing over at the tired figure in her kitchen, and shoved a couple things around, before bringing out a small, white, spiral tablet of lined paper and a pencil. She came back to the table, wrote on the open page and ripped it out quickly, which caused Cheryl to jump and look up through her misery.

Mrs. A handed her the paper. Without looking at it, Cheryl pleaded, "Come with me." Mrs. A stiffened, but Cheryl didn't seem to notice. "I can't ask anyone else. And I can't go alone. Please." She was begging, but she didn't know what she was asking.

"First you call the number. It's for the Planned Parenthood Clinic in Highland Park. You'll need an appointment. Don't lie. Don't make it worse. Do what you have to do. I will be right here. But you need to make the call."

"I'll do it right now. Where's your phone?" Cheryl was looking around, afraid to lose her momentum. She saw the phone on the kitchen wall. She rushed over to it, grabbed the receiver, and dialed the numbers. She looked scared, but she didn't stop. "I need an appointment," she stammered. "Yeah, that's right." She looked over at Mrs. A. "Yeah, I'm sure. What? Last May." She paused, listening. "What? Oh, crap! No, I'm sorry. I just didn't think. Okay." Again, she waited.

"When? So soon? Sure. Yeh. Sure. Cheryl. Thanks. Bye." She hung up the phone. "Thursday, at ten. Will you come?" It was a simple question simply asked. It was a horrendous question simply asked.

* * * * *

Usually, the girls stayed with her until..., until things were settled. But they had to let their parents know, that is, if they were still with their parents. So many were thrown out when their pregnancies were discovered.

"Do you need a place to stay?"

"Yes," Cheryl whispered. "Please."

"Do your parents know?"

"My mom, not my dad."

"Can you go home and get some things?"

"I guess." Cheryl looked at the clock. "My dad won't be home until almost six."

"Okay then. You have to tell your mom you're with me."

"No! She can't know I've come to you."

"But...," Mrs. A said.

"They don't.... They won't help me. They'd kill me first."

"Cheryl, really. 'Kill' you?"

"Really! They're very against.... Things...."

* * * * *

Chapter 2

After Cheryl left, Mrs. A remembered when her granddaughter, Cate had been to visit before her prom. A beautiful, healthy, athletic teenager dressed in basketball sweats that couldn't really hide her young, strong, confident body. Her shoes were big and clunky. "High tops," she called them. Her hair was tied in messy knots. Her bright smile was in the middle of a scrubbed face with a touch of makeup at the eyes making them look even more wide open and innocent. She was so excited. She was going to prom.

"I asked a boy in orchestra. He sits second chair in second violins. So we talk a lot. You knew I was first chair viola, right Grandma? So, we sit next to each other."

She had nodded, although it was hard to remember what they all were doing. She didn't want to interfere with the words that bubbled up from this refreshing brook of a granddaughter. Let her run like she was meant to run. Full stream ahead. The words floating down and cascading over little rock shelves in the sunlight of excitement.

"Since January. Trang moved to St. Paul and I moved up. No audition, just shift. I suppose I could've asked him too. Oh well, I didn't think of it. Jay was so handy. And we talk a lot now."

"When is it?"

"Next month. End of May."

"Do you have a dress yet?" she asked sipping her Diet Rite.

"Oh my gosh!" she bubbled. "It's so cool! Not strapless. Mom said, 'Not strapless!' But I tried them on anyway. And she was right. I tried dancing in it, and it stayed put, but I danced out! Too funny! Jess and I had a ball. Trying on dresses, and coming out, showing each other, dancing with no music. Sometimes we called each other 'uuughleee.' Well, some of the dresses were sooo bad. We looked like Cinderella's stepsisters. We laughed sooo hard. There were girls there from other schools too. But they were too cool to laugh and kept looking at us like we were crazy. Jess is so much fun! She's going with a guy named Alex, he's third trumpet and plays baseball. We're double dating. Dinner at 'the Inn.' Photos at my and her house. Anyway, you know I don't date. Anyone! But who can pass up their prom. So, I asked him. He didn't know at first, but I told him what my mom said. I didn't tell him that she said it. But I told him that it would be like a costume party. We go all fancied up and just have fun. Play dress-up! Act grown up! Well, maybe not. Grown up, I mean."

She hopped off the chair and whirled around the kitchen. Then started swinging her arms and stomping about in what Mrs. A supposed was the current dance craze. She whirled back and hung one arm on her grandma's shoulder and squeezed in a quick time hug that transmitted joy and fun to the older woman. Then she shot an imaginary basket and plunked herself back down.

After she had gone, the air was still fresh with the torrent of Cate's words. What a difference between Cate's and Cheryl's proms.

Mrs. A stayed at the table, elbows braced to hold her Diet Rite, shoulders hunched. What a joy Cate was. Had Mrs. A ever been that carefree? Not for a long time, if ever. "Oh well," Mrs. A gave a big sigh, Cheryl was certainly not "carefree" anymore.

Chapter 3

Despite Cheryl's appearance in her kitchen, Mrs. A was excited. This was the day. A beautiful day. Fall wasn't yet in the air. The school year hadn't started. She was only having one guest for tea, but she was special. A tiny girl, her sister's great granddaughter, Mia's granddaughter, was coming to tea. A tea party! Just the two of them. Cozy and fun. Combining the ages. Bridging the gap.

There had been many tea parties before. In fact, Mrs. Anderson, or Mrs. A as she was called when not Mom or Grandma, was proud of her reputation for tea parties. All the little girls (and a couple little boys) had learned to be quiet and polite and, well, a little serious at tea with her. There were always moments of giggles and, often, great outbursts of laughter, which were fought down with major efforts in respect for the "event," the tea party.

Coming out of the kitchen, she checked once more to see if she had forgotten anything. She had the tea set that she had been given as a little girl. And her little table and chairs.

She moved the pink roses, the last from her garden, around in the little vase, but they had their own way of standing and would not be arranged. Taking her apron off, she went back into the kitchen.

Her guest was named Rachel and she had dark hair, deep dark brown eyes, and long fingers. Rachel loved to pretend. She especially loved to pretend with Mrs. A, one of the adults in her life who took time for her and loved her.

Rachel was four, and Mrs. A, really her great aunt, had known Rachel since she was born. Her mother Lisa was Mia's daughter. She had been adopted by a friend of Mrs. A's. It was all "hush-hush" at the time, and Rachel knew Mrs. A as a friend of the family. They didn't see each other very often, but when Rachel's mother, Lisa, had a doctor's appointment, Mrs. A invited Rachel to tea.

The doorbell rang and Mrs. A gave a quick approving look at the tea table and a quick forgiving look at herself in the mirror. She patted her tight golden red curls to make sure her hairdo was in place, and she moved her hands down the front of her dress to smooth out the wrinkles.

She opened the door and glanced with a quick smile at the still slim Lisa standing on her stoop. But she reserved her widest, most welcoming smile for the little girl half hiding behind Lisa. The little girl was quite a picture with her red hat crunched onto her head, her denim coveralls over a white blouse, her khaki jacket, and shiny, patent leather Mary Janes. Rachel was choking a bear very tightly, in case he might run away. Mrs. A bubbled with joy as she asked them to "Please come in. I'm so glad to see you all." She backed away to the side so Lisa and Rachel and the bear, it appeared to be a koala, could come into her house. Standing at the door, she looked up and down the street and noticed the car parked across the street with a woman holding a notepad and a pencil and glancing up at the house.

Lisa was saying, "It's so great that you can do this. I didn't know anyone else to call. I'll only be gone an hour or two. Do you think you can manage? Rachel, you be a big girl and help Mrs. A. Love you! Well, I'd better run. I'm sure it will be good news. But we'll have to see. You understand. Bye! Bye, Rachel Bug!" And she was out the door, hurrying down the walk to her car. Rachel and Mrs. A watched her open her car door and wave her hand out the window as she drove off down the street.

* * * * * * *

Mrs. A got down on one knee so that she was closer in size to the little Rachel. "I see you've brought a friend," she said. "What do you call your bear?"

"Koly," Rachel whispered. "'Cause he's a 'kola' bear. He's from 'Astrayla.'" Her little voice got louder as she mispronounced the continent.

"My, you do have to hug him tight don't you? Will he run away do you think?" asked Mrs. A.

"He's stuffed," said Rachel matter-of-factly, "he can't run."

"I guess you're right," chuckled Mrs. A.

"My mom said we were going to have a tea party?". She still hadn't moved from the door.

Mrs. A chuckled again and said, "That's for sure. I have it almost ready. Would you like to see?" Rachel nodded and followed her farther into the room, around the couch, where she saw the little table and two chairs.

Mrs. A said, "Just a minute. I have to find a chair for Koly. I wasn't expecting two guests for tea. But what a pleasure to have you both." She went into another room, returned with a small doll's highchair and placed it next to the table. Then she went out again.

When Mrs. A came back this time, she had a little cup and saucer, plate, napkin, and spoon that matched those already on the table. She placed the dishes and things in front of the highchair on the table. "You can set Koly in the highchair, I think it will suit him well," she offered.

Rachel stuffed Koly into the chair and scolded, "Now you be good! Or else!"

"Why don't you sit there where you can keep an eye on him," suggested Mrs. A pointing at the chair closest to the highchair. She pulled out the little chair on the other side and eased herself down carefully so that her knees didn't bump the table. She tucked her legs and feet back and under so that she actually looked comfortable sitting on the small chair at the small table.

'Tea?" asked Mrs. A.

"What's tea?" said Rachel.

"Oh," Mrs. A breathed, "it's something to drink. People all over the world drink tea. But it's more than a drink for people. It's always been a special time with people sitting together drinking tea. Having tea is a proper activity and we have to behave with our best manners, you know. The water must be very hot to make the tea, so we have to be careful or someone could be burned and that wouldn't feel very good would it?"

Rachel looked up from the tea kettle into the older woman's bright eyes and murmured, "We'll be good."

Mrs. A opened a tin. It was square and brightly colored with gold on the rim and edges. "The tea is in this tin. Today we're having Earl Grey tea. There are many kinds of tea." Some are even used as medicine. She spooned some tea into the pink rose pot with the silver rim. Rachel saw the little dark pieces fall off the spoon into the pot.

"What is that?" she asked with her eyebrows close together and her nose a little wrinkled as she looked at the strange stuff.

"It's little pieces of leaves that have been dried and broken. When I pour the hot water over the leaves, the flavor will mix with the water and the smell will rise up with the steam. It's really quite wonderful," Mrs. A explained. She poured the water into the little teapot and set the kettle back onto its trivet.

"Now," she said, "We'll let the tea steep a little and chat." She picked up her little rose-colored napkin and shook it open. Watching Rachel, she laid it across her lap. "Wouldn't want to spill on our clothes, would we?" she said. Rachel took her own napkin, almost taking her plate with it. Mrs. A didn't seem to notice. Rachel shook her napkin open too and laid it in a pile on her little lap.

Mrs. A offered, "We should tie Koly's napkin around his neck so he can't wiggle out from under and get his fur and vest dirty." She reached over and quickly tied a napkin behind Koly's neck and he was pronounced "ready–set–go" for tea.

"Oh my goodness!" Mrs. A gasped. "I've forgotten my hat." And reaching behind her she picked up a straw hat with a green scarf tied around it, hanging down. A pink rose stuck into the scarf where it went around the hat. Looking at it carefully to find the front and back, she plopped the hat on top of her golden red curls and said, "Now that's more proper!" Then she handed Rachel a flowered hat which she somberly placed on Koly's head. On her own head, she still wore her own red hat.

"Dear Rachel," began Mrs. A, "now for a chat. How are you? I'm fine, thank you. So happy you could join me for tea. I haven't seen you for ages. How's your family? What have you been up to?"

Rachel shrank a little shorter into her chair.

"Are you married yet?" asked Mrs. A. Rachel laughed.

"Oh, of course not," said Mrs. A. "You're not even out of school yet. How silly of me," she laughed.

"I'm not even in school yet," giggled Rachel. "I go to nursery school some days. There's lots of kids there. It's fun.

"Good for you. School should be fun. I think the tea may be ready," guessed Mrs. A. "May I pour you some?" she said holding up the teapot.

Rachel nodded. "Umm, sure."

Mrs. A poured some into Rachel's cup and then Koly's cup and lastly, she poured her own cup. She placed the teapot on the table and said, "Sugar? One lump or two?" and raised her eyebrows at Rachel.

"What?" asked Rachel, puzzled.

"I take my tea with one lump of sugar. So why don't you try it that way too?" she explained.

She picked up a little square piece of sugar with a little tong and dropped it into Rachel's cup and then did the same thing for Koly and herself. She stirred her tea with a tiny spoon and Rachel copied her, enjoying the clinking of the spoon against the cup.

"Let's taste it," Mrs. A suggested after a while, picking up her little cup and holding it with her little finger curved up and away. Rachel looked at Mrs. A's cup and finger and tried to do the same.

Mrs. A lifted a napkin off the plate that was in the center of the table and revealed some chocolate covered cookies that had been hiding there. Rachel took one cookie. And then she said, "Can Koly have one too?" Mrs. A nodded and Rachel plunked one on Koly's plate. She planned to help Koly eat his.

"I'm so glad you could come by. And I hope you will enjoy coming again. More tea?" And she held the teapot up and raised one eyebrow in a question.

Rachel answered very properly, "Yes, please." And Mrs. A poured the tea and said "One lump or two?" And they clinked their spoons and sipped and Rachel finished her cookie and helped Koly eat his.

* * * * * * *

After tea, they sat on the couch together and read books. Rachel was "reading" to Mrs. A when the doorbell "ding-donged" and Mrs. A said, "That must be your mother. Let's see how things went for her." She and Rachel went to the door and opened it.

Rachel's mother, Lisa, was standing on the stoop. She was smiling and said, "Everything's fine, in fact it's great!"

"So, you're expecting!" said Mrs. A, giving Lisa a squeeze on her arm. "I'm so glad for you. Do you have a date?"

"Yes," chimed Lisa. "The middle of February, maybe Valentine's Day. A little bundle of love for us."

Rachel was tugging at Lisa's jacket, needing attention. "Did you have a good time, Rachel bug?" asked her mother.

"We had tea," Rachel answered smiling shyly at Mrs. A. "With one lump."

"That's good dear. There's nothing like tea with Mrs. A. I like my tea with one lump too," Lisa said. "We'd better be getting home though. Thank you so much for watching her. Can I count on you next month too?" Lisa asked. "I have to go every month now."

Mrs. Anderson replied soothingly. "Of course. I enjoyed it and I think Rachel had a good time too, didn't you Rachel?"

"Uh huh," answered Rachel, nodding her head.

Rachel turned to leave with her mother, but, after a few steps, she spun around in a panic and ran past Mrs. A into the house.

Very soon she was back with her bear. She held him up so Mrs. A could take off the napkin they had tied around his neck. "Koly says thank you," Rachel said. As Mrs. A leaned down to pat Koly, Rachel kissed her cheek. "Rachel says thank you too. Bye! And say goodbye to that girl for me." And off she ran down the walk behind her mother to the car. She waved out the window as they drove away past the woman in the parked car.

* * * * * * *

Mrs. A turned back into the house and went over to take away the tea dishes until the next time. She saw Cheryl curled up in her husband's large leather wingback chair. An athletic bag in the high school colors was thrown up against the leg of the chair.

"You made good time," she said to the girl. Angry, determined eyes glared back at her. "What have you told your family?"

"They don't care! And I don't give a damn about them!" Cheryl jumped up and grabbed her bag, hefting it over her shoulder, ready to march like the soldiers on the TV boarding the planes for Vietnam.

After she had settled Cheryl into the spare bedroom, Mrs. A relaxed with some more tea. She was thinking of Kelly who had been in the tenth grade when she had had her abortion. Of course, she had lost touch with her. She was able to follow her high school years through articles in the paper and from listening to neighbors and friends. Sometimes she would see her on the street. Kelly always looked away, turned away, hurried on. Things had gone well during high school. But not in college. She dropped out. Had come back and was working in a local bank. Cashiering. She looked so efficient. Mrs. A would come in and see her smiling at the customers, chatting with her fellow workers. She heard there was another man in her life. They were living together. Going to get married. She saw her one day and she looked pregnant. Then she heard that the baby had been born dead, the cord wrapped around his neck. Mrs. A mourned for that baby too. She sent Kelly a sympathy note and wrote that she was sorry for her "losses" – and it wasn't a mistake.

This memory made her think of her son, Andrew, same age as Kelly. He was a doctor now, living in Chicago. He had found out from some girls at school, that his mother was the one who "helped." She was "the one to go to. The one to "fix it."" He had gotten angry. So angry, he could hardly face her. He coped by detaching totally from her, abandoning her emotionally. He wouldn't allow her to do anything for him. He did his own laundry, cleaning, cooking. He wouldn't join the family for meals or any activities. She knew he had talked with his dad, but Al was unresponsive, as usual, when she asked about the talk. Her husband always denied knowledge or acquiescence in her activities. Andrew was gone more than he was home during the rest of high school. And when he went to college, he had found one far away and had never returned, not for summers, not for holidays, not after graduation.

* * * * * * *

Mrs. A turned back into the house and went over to take away the tea dishes until the next time. She saw Cheryl curled up in her husband's large leather wingback chair. An athletic bag in the high school colors was thrown up against the leg of the chair.

"You made good time," she said to the girl. Angry, determined eyes glared back at her. "What have you told your family?"

"They don't care! And I don't give a damn about them!" Cheryl jumped up and grabbed her bag, hefting it over her shoulder, ready to march like the soldiers on the TV boarding the planes for Vietnam.

After she had settled Cheryl into the spare bedroom, Mrs. A relaxed with some more tea. She was thinking of Kelly who had been in the tenth grade when she had had her abortion. Of course, she had lost touch with her. She was able to follow her high school years through articles in the paper and from listening to neighbors and friends. Sometimes she would see her on the street. Kelly always looked away, turned away, hurried on. Things had gone well during high school. But not in college. She dropped out. Had come back and was working in a local bank. Cashiering. She looked so efficient. Mrs. A would come in and see her smiling at the customers, chatting with her fellow workers. She heard there was another man in her life. They were living together. Going to get married. She saw her one day and she looked pregnant. Then she heard that the baby had been born dead, the cord wrapped around his neck. Mrs. A mourned for that baby too. She sent Kelly a sympathy note and wrote that she was sorry for her "losses" – and it wasn't a mistake.

This memory made her think of her son, Andrew, same age as Kelly. He was a doctor now, living in Chicago. He had found out from some girls at school, that his mother was the one who "helped." She was "the one to go to. The one to "fix it."" He had gotten angry. So angry, he could hardly face her. He coped by detaching totally from her, abandoning her emotionally. He wouldn't allow her to do anything for him. He did his own laundry, cleaning, cooking. He wouldn't join the family for meals or any activities. She knew he had talked with his dad, but Al was unresponsive, as usual, when she asked about the talk. Her husband always denied knowledge or acquiescence in her activities. Andrew was gone more than he was home during the rest of high school. And when he went to college, he had found one far away and had never returned, not for summers, not for holidays, not after graduation.

* * * * * * *

Al wouldn't ask. She would say "I have to…" and he would go along with her needs. He'd do whatever she asked or wanted. He had been great about the kids. Always there for them when she couldn't be. He wanted no explanation. He never let her get into it with him. He must have been able to tell when she wanted or needed to talk and he would move away, change the subject, or hug her, but never let her talk. Was he afraid he couldn't stop what might begin if they talked about it? Was it "woman stuff?" He never wanted to hear about that sort of thing. Did he disapprove? Was he disgusted? Or angry?

It didn't matter, that's the way it was. He was the only one she could have talked with about it, but he wouldn't. So, it was all in her. It was not their life. It was her's. It separated them. And finally, he had left. He had found a life with

Shirley, a woman less challenging. They traveled and did many things together, but nothing serious got in their way. They learned ballroom dancing together and loved to waltz through life. He deserved that, but Mrs. A couldn't waltz through her life. Her dance floor wasn't smooth and clean and uncrowded. He managed much better with Shirley on her dance floor.

And there had been Ben. Not much talking there either. But there was understanding. They worked with each other. He helped her girls. Mrs. A would contact him, and he performed the procedures. In the hospital. A "D & C." Because of some "complication." It was so normal for them to come together over their "secret." And they physically and emotionally comforted each other. Their spouses never knew and therefore, no one was hurt. Really.

Chapter 4

"Hey! It's been too long! Look at you!" Ginny's voice was confident and possessive. It may have been months between visits, but she and Mrs. A still belonged together. They were still a unit. A unit of two very different parts, but the connection never broke.

"I can't believe it!" gasped Mrs. A, looking over the street for the ever-present car. "How I've missed you! Come in! Need something to drink?" Her hug was received with a broad grin.

"Just water," Ginny replied. Her short, dusty colored hair curved back around her ears, but fell lazily over her forehead. She had the pear shaped body versus Mrs. A's apple shape. She was a ten on top and an eighteen on the bottom. Both equally lamented. Her height was medium, her demeanor strong. Her hands and fingers were constantly moving, "to keep 'Arthur' at bay," she would say. That also explained why she was always crocheting something wonderful and useful to give away.

"Come on in the kitchen. Just put your bag there. Do you need the bathroom?"

"Not yet. I emptied out and filled up at a gas station up the road. Oh, thanks," she said as Mrs. A set a big glass of ice water on the table in front of her. She lowered herself onto the chair and put her big crushable bag on the table with a resonating clunk, almost knocking the entire glass over, but managing a last minute save that resulted only in a small puddle quickly absorbed by the napkin Mrs. A tossed on it.

"Same old klutz, eh?" Ginny sighed.

"That's the you I love," Mrs. A laughed. "This time it was just a little mess."

"Yeah, thanks for the small ones. Such a humongous bag, but I guess I need it all."

"Yeh, really?" Mrs. A questioned sarcastically. "How's it going?

"Same," Ginny answered. Numbers were her realm, not words. She had been a math teacher before she retired. The two friends were the same age, but Ginny had continued teaching after her kids were born.

"Everyone healthy?" Mrs. A continued.

"Yeh, it's been a good year. Mom's still going strong."

"And the kids?" Mrs. A asked.

"Haven't heard anything. We're having Bryan's next week. Mike's were last weekend. That Suzy is a handful. Whooo!"

"What happened this time?" Mrs. A asked, hoping for a good story.

"You can't even 'time out' her. She sits in the corner chanting 'I'm in time out! I'm in time out!' She's a challenge."

"Yeah, she's a busy one. Gotta love her," laughed Mrs. A.

The kitchen door opened and Cheryl started to enter. She stopped short when she saw Ginny.

"No, come on in. Cheryl this is my friend Ginny. Cheryl is spending a few days with me."

"Hello," Cheryl said shyly. The fire burning her up had been dampened for a while. She was just a kid in the kitchen with two older women who were very comfortable with each other.

"Hello, take a load off," Ginny said, patting the chair next to her. "Are you one of Marion's lost lambs?" she asked bluntly. Cheryl looked pale and worried.

"Take it easy, Gin. Let the girl get to know us a little before you put her on the spot. Ginny and I go back a long way. We first met in seventh grade."

"Yeah, I was too rowdy."

"And I was too square," Mrs. A responded. "Still am," she laughed. "So, we didn't connect right away."

"I told a dirty joke and Marion was such a prude then."

"Still am!" Mrs. A laughed again. "So, we knew each other a long time without really being friends."

"Things must have changed," Cheryl surmised shyly.

"Ginny rescued me in college. All my friends had gone away to college and Ginny took me in."

"I just offered her a ride to the 'U.' My Dad was driving a bunch of us. And Marion was taking the bus," Ginny explained.

"After that she couldn't get rid of me," Mrs. A chuckled.

"Well, you proved to be useful."

"Yeah, she even asked me to stand up for her. Anyway, they say 'opposites attract.'" Mrs. A clinked glasses with her best friend.

"That's us!" Ginny agreed.

The phone rang. With a glance at the other two, Mrs. A got up to answer it. She moved away from them.

Ginny asked, "Do you go to the high school here?"

"Yeh," Cheryl responded.

"What grade?" Ginny inquired sipping her drink.

Cheryl walked over to the refrigerator, took out some orange juice, retrieved a glass from the cupboard and poured some. As she started to put the juice back, she remembered her manners. "Want some?" she asked, raising the container.

"Nah, water's fine. Thanks anyway," Ginny answered. "What grade?" she asked again.

"Twelfth," Cheryl said looking over the rim of her glass as she sipped her juice. "I didn't mean to interrupt," she said edging her way to the door. "Tell Mrs. A I'm going to watch TV upstairs, ok?"

"Sure. Take it easy." Ginny watched Cheryl back out of the door with her juice.

Ginny turned back to Mrs. A, who was still talking on the phone, but was facing her with more than worry on her face.

"Ginny's here for the weekend. Yes, my friend Ginny. For the weekend. Yes, the whole weekend." Putting her hand over the phone, she said, "It's Mia. Something's happened. She needs to come over. Cate too."

Ginny raised her hands to question, but Mrs. A responded "Don't know. Do you mind?"

"Nah, I can make myself scarce – or not – maybe I can help," said Ginny.

Mrs. A looked doubtful and queried the phone, "When will you get here? Oh, okay. Dinner? No? Well, we'll see. See you soon then. Love ya!"

She hung the phone up with a puzzled, worried look and said, "It's something awful. She wouldn't say what. You know how she gets. You can't budge her. Well, we'll have to see."

"When's she coming?" Ginny asked.

"Now."

* * * * * * *

When the doorbell rang, Mrs. A jumped and dumped a little of her water on the floor.

"Now what?" she wondered out loud. She threw a napkin over the spill and swished it around with her foot. "It can't be them already." She threw the napkin in the garbage can. Shaking her head, she went through the swinging door.

As she walked through the living room. She saw the remains of the tea party she hadn't cleared away yet. It seemed a long time ago that she and Rachel had spent such a wonderful, loving time together.

Reaching the door, she smoothed her front and looked at the mirror with a frown of disapproval. When she opened the door, she was attacked with great hugs from two young women who were babbling with excitement.

"Look who's here!" cried Lisa.

"You look great!" shouted the other.

"Nancy! Oh my gosh! What's going on? It's been so long! Wha…?" Mrs. A was laughing and hugging them both back.

"Isn't it great! She surprised me. When I got home with Rachel, there she was having coffee with Sean." They kept talking, each in rapid succession, hardly waiting for the other to finish.

Nancy explained, "I didn't call, because she's always so busy and can't get together, or so she says. I just showed up. And then I hear the great news."

"What great news?" Ginny asked, coming from the kitchen with her water.

"Lisa's 'pg!'" stated Nancy at the same time Lisa sighed happily, "I'm pregnant."

The two young women rushed into the room, dropping their purses near the couch. They gave Ginny quick hugs along with greetings and then flowed through the swinging kitchen door, one after the other, still laughing and chattering.

Ginny and Mrs. A looked at each other. Ginny commented, "Oh my! Were we ever that young?"

"Absolutely! And just as noisy. Why else did my mom call you the 'blond bombshell?'"

They followed the younger women back into the kitchen and found they had already made themselves at home with coffee and cookies they found in the cupboard.

The laughter and exclamations attracted Cheryl as she stuck her head into the room, peaking around the swinging door.

"Come in, Cheryl. Meet some more wonderful people. This is Nancy, my cousin Carol's daughter…."

"Adopted!" interrupted Lisa and then she and Nancy burst into laughter.

Mrs. A smiled permissibly. "And this is my friend, Lisa. She's the mother of the little girl who was here for tea."

"Yeh, I saw her before. Hi," she added softly.

"This is Cheryl. She'll be staying here a while," finished Mrs. A. "Oh, and you two remember Ginny, my college friend?"

"Sure."

"Yeh. Who could forget?" responded Nancy.

And Ginny answered, "It's been a long time."

"But you haven't changed much," Lisa tried to compliment the older woman.

"Thanks," Ginny said, "but you two have – changed, I mean."

"Isn't it great? We're both into families, kids, and jobs and it's all so exciting," said Lisa.

"And damned hard," added Nancy. "Who the hell said 'women could have it all' should be shot."

"Amen!" added Ginny.

Mrs. A laughed, raising her hand as if guilty. "Well, we meant the opportunity, the choice. To have it all. We want options. For everyone. Men. Women. Stay home. Work. Do it all. You can't blame us if the world just widened the slave ship so both men and women could man the oars."

"Thar she blows!" Ginny warned, continuing the metaphor. "Give her an opening...."

"Don't we know it!" exclaimed Nancy. "There were times we were so glad she left. She'd get so wound up, you couldn't even ignore her."

"Ignore me? Is that what you did?"

"We heard you," Lisa soothed. "Even if you thought we weren't listening. We just didn't believe you. Until...."

"Yeh. Until the boom fell on us and we knew it when it happened, because of you. Because of how you would carry on. You made it easy to recognize the bullshit, pardon my French, but what could we do? You obviously didn't solve the problems or we wouldn't have felt the boom," Nancy continued.

"What a couple of whiners!" Ginny exhaled. "Ya do what ya gottta do."

"Especially once there are kids," said Mrs. A.

"Or before," quipped Ginny.

Cheryl kept looking from one to the other as the conversation racketed around the room. A look of confusion and wonderment covered her puzzled face. The two older and the two younger women laughed and continued their conversation which took many tacks and ebbed and flowed, splashed with laughter.

When the doorbell rang again, only Mrs. A heard it. She slid off her chair and worked her way around the counter to the door. She slipped through just as the others finally noticed.

Nancy said to Ginny, "What's up? She looked worried."

"Mia and Cate are stopping by. Marion said it sounded serious."

"Mia and Cate?" questioned Cheryl.

"Marion's daughter Mia and her daughter Cate," answered Ginny.

"She has two daughters?" asked Cheryl.

"Nah," Ginny responded. "I said it wrong – nothing unusual there. Cate is Mia's daughter and Marion's granddaughter. Actually, she is named after Marion's daughter Kathrine, so sure, she has two daughters, Kathrine and Mia. And Cate is her granddaughter. Mia's daughter. Is that clear?"

"As mud!" laughed Nancy.

No one was coming into the kitchen, and they could hear murmuring through the door. After a while Ginny said, "Enough of this." And started toward the door. The others looked shocked at her forwardness. But Ginny continued through the door and into the conversation occurring in the living room. The others hurried behind her.

* * * * * * *

Mrs. A's daughter Mia had turned out "all right." She had come to stay shortly after Karen, Mia's mother and Mrs. A's sister, had…died. So had Karen's boys, Bob and Randy. The boys had been older. Sixteen and fourteen. Mia had been only eleven. Bill, their dad, couldn't "handle it." They were "too much." It was "too hard." He'd pay. He didn't. He'd visit. He did, but rarely.

It was too hard for Mrs. A too. Her sister was gone. She had her own family, the kids, Katherine and Andrew, and her husband Al. A traditional family, she ran the home and he ran his business. Their house was small, but they converted the den for Karen's boys and Mia moved in with Katherine. Andrew was allowed his own room, because he was older and needed the space for his projects and studies. Katherine was twelve, not that much older than Mia. But the trauma of Karen's death had shattered Mia's life so that she could hardly function. At first the girls shared a bed, but Mia's bedwetting put a stop to that and then they squeezed another bed into the already small room. Although, often, in the night, Mrs. A, when she couldn't sleep and the tears of loss wouldn't stop, would find Mia curled up next to the sleeping Katherine, not really touching, but almost. She would carefully lift her back into her own bed, and those nights her bed would be dry in the morning.

Mia didn't talk much. She watched every thing, but didn't do much in the beginning. Mrs. A kept her close. At first, after the others headed off to school, she kept her home. She would direct her play and have her help with the chores. She talked to her, read her books, sang to her and took her along on errands. When she ran into people she knew, she always introduced her as her niece. For a while that was enough, but eventually that changed and Mia became her "daughter." Mia didn't like to hug or play rough. You could pat her and compliment her. And she was a good girl, quickly adjusting and heading off to school with the other kids.

Katherine had problems sharing. So, the room was divided by an imaginary line. And it worked well too. With their natures, there was a great deal of difference in toys and activities. Mia was quick and, by watching what was going on, she began to fit in with the family routine. Katherine's friends found Mia amusing and loved to tease her and liked to include her in their activities which made Katherine jealous. Eventually, those friends didn't come around much. Katherine played at her friends' houses or at home alone.

The boys got along fine. Bob and Randy had each other and their sports and friends. They were polite, ate great amounts of food, and cleaned their room when they were told. They liked to watch sports on TV with Al, who was grateful for their company. They were kind to their little sister and pretty much ignored Katherine. Andrew, at seventeen, was content that they were busy and didn't need a lot of time from him. He had his music, and his projects.

There were the usual difficulties. Who got to watch what when? Who got to be first or sit by the window in the car? Why did one get a bigger piece? The TV had been moved to the basement, so Andrew could practice the piano, which couldn't be moved to the basement. The sports fans didn't mind the centipedes and spiders, but the girls did. It was understood that practice was necessary. TV was not. And Andrew loved to practice. He never had to be reminded. And he could play for hours. No griping. No battles like with Katherine and her lessons.

Karen, the beautiful mother and sister. The too young bride swept off her feet by the handsome Bill. The two boys and then the two "miscarriages" before Mia was born. Mrs. A would watch the boys for a weekend away for Bill and Karen. Later Karen would tell Mrs. A that she was no longer pregnant.

But it was different when she was pregnant with Mia. Karen seemed so happy but wouldn't talk about why. She was dieting and exercising like mad, she said for the high school reunion coming up. Nothing about a pregnancy. Then she showed up with a bruised face and said she had fallen helping Bill get the boat ready before he left on his fishing trip. Mrs. A had already noticed the string holding Karen's pants together over her swelling tummy, but she had been too wary to ask if she was pregnant. She just stared at her sister and the bruise. Her shock and amazement were too much for Karen, who cried out. "So what! It's a small price to pay!" They collapsed into each other's arms and wept. Mrs. A finally asked softly, "Will he come back?"

"I think so. But I know this has to be the last one. I just couldn't do it again. I felt so bad those other times. And it was so dirty. Filthy! The whole thing. The lying. The haggling over money. I was so alone. He waited in the car after he paid. I couldn't go through it again!"

"But…" Mrs. A stuttered. "But how? Who took care of you? What about the pain? You could've been sterilized!"

"That would have been the greatest! You know, you need a committee to okay that kind of procedure. And you know how dependable that damn rhythm is. He wouldn't let me use a diaphragm. Wouldn't think of a rubber. Didn't feel 'natural.' So it happened again. And I waited to tell him. I couldn't do it again. I miss those babies so much. I think about them all the time. What they would be doing now? How they would look? I don't even know if they were boys or girls. So, I waited. And when he figured it out, he was furious. Said I betrayed him. Said it wasn't his. Said he would never accept it. I never said a word. Then he hit me and left. I don't know if he'll be back. He took the boat. It was all loaded for the lake. I don't know." She had released her sister and was wiping her eyes in an effort to get control of herself. Control was what she needed. She had two kids and one on the way. That much was certain. That and the fact that her sister would understand and help her. And he had come back. And Mia had been born. And she got pregnant again. And the beloved sister, Karen, mother of three, no five, had jumped off the High Bridge.

* * * * * * *

Mrs. A, Mia, and Ginny ended up on kitchen duty once the pizza delivery was enjoyed and everyone had cried "enough."

"Well, that was easy," declared Mrs. A closing the fridge door.

"Aren't you glad I insisted on paper plates?" Ginny responded.

"You're always right and I'm always too up tight. But you know I like to set a pretty table."

"You did. The fruit and veggies really added color and the checked napkins were perfection.

"Yeh. Mom always tries to be Betty Crocker." Mia's voice wasn't very relaxed.

"So," Ginny turned to her and said, "What's the deal? Your call has me on needles and your mom is worried sick."

"Pins. You mean, pins and needles. And, I am not! Concerned. Yes. That was a strange call. And I can tell something's going on. Cate has hardly said a word, Mrs. A said."

"Well, you don't make things easy, as usual." Mia's voice was now snide. She peeked through the door and turned to continue. "They're pretty quiet in there. Who the hell is this Cheryl? One of your 'girls?' I should have known you'd have one of them here when I needed you." Tears ran down her face and her body sagged back into the kitchen and onto a chair.

Mrs. A came around the table as Ginny reached over to Mia's knee. Mrs. A tried to gather her daughter into her arms, but Mia stiffened and cried "Don't! It will only make it harder."

Mrs. A stepped back, but kept her arms open in an attempt to comfort the desperate woman. Ginny's hand remained on Mia's knee.

Mia straightened and ignoring the open embrace and the firm hand, she gulped, "Cate is…pregnant."

"Well, we already knew that," Ginny responded, slapping Mia's knee as she took her hand away.

"What? How?" Mia was shocked.

Ginny explained. "Her face, her clothes, her attitude – not good by the way. She's not the same young woman I saw last spring. Going on and on about the prom."

"She's got a beautiful glow. She looks just like you when you were pregnant. But she's so sad." Mrs. A crooned and tried again to hug her.

Mia shook off her mother's arm and stood. "Well then, you know. So, what do we do?"

"Is this the time to talk about it?" Mrs. A wondered.

"Why not?" Ginny asked.

"Well, when I called, I told Cate Ginny was here."

"Obviously she didn't care, 'cause she's here," Ginny stated

"Yeah, but the others? I don't know how she feels about that," Mia sighed.

"Well, if not now, when? We might as well go in and see how the land lays…, lies," Ginny said, grabbing Mia's arm and heading toward the door.

A terrified Mia looked back at her mother.

"I'm right behind you," Mrs. A smiled back at her.

* * * * * * *

The others all looked up as the three women came into the living room. They were looking through some photo albums that Mrs. A always left on the coffee table. Family pictures. Family vacations. Family events. She had one just devoted to her sister, Karen, but that one was in her bedroom. Saved for private times and memories.

Cheryl's eyes narrowed as she sat on the arm of the couch, ready to fight or flee if she had to. Cate curled up even tighter in her grandpa's old leather chair. Lisa and Nancy sat on the floor near the coffee table leaning over the books, pointing at pictures and remembering and trying very hard to get Cate to join in. They were talking in voices loud enough for Cheryl and Cate to hear, but not loud enough to be heard from the kitchen. They didn't notice the three until Ginny plunked down on the couch next to Cheryl.

"How ya doing, Hon?" she asked patting her on the thigh. "Getting to know these gals?"

"Oh, that's true," Mrs. A added. "They've known each other their whole lives." She looked around the group and then back to Cheryl. "This is

Cheryl. She came today and will be staying awhile. Should we tell them why you're here?"

Mia exclaimed, "Oh, we know why. Sure, you're one of the 'girls.' Everyone knows about 'Mrs. A's girls' anyway. We've met a lot of them over the years. Oh, am I wrong?" She stopped abruptly as she saw the horrified look on her mother's face.

Cheryl's face blanched as they all looked at her. Her quiet response was almost not heard at first. But her voice got a bit stronger as she felt the warmth of the women in the room.

"Yes, I mean, no, you're not wrong, I think. I mean, I know about Mrs. A and how she can help. I don't know what I'm going to do. But I know she will help me, no matter what I decide. The kids at school – we all kind of know. Some friends thought I should check it out." Her voice trailed off. She looked down at her hands.

"How far along are you?" Mia almost snarled.

Cate's back straightened a little and she flushed a miserable red. She stared at the other girl. She glanced at her mother and grandmother and then continued her inspection of Cheryl.

"Three, four maybe. I'm starting to look it. I think everyone can see. I can't keep going to school. I'm afraid my mom knows and my Dad will find out. I'm scared to go home. So, I'm here!" Cheryl's tone had increased in intensity and defiance. When she stopped, she was surprised that she was standing in front of the group with her hands on her hips, glaring at nothing in particular, but taking everyone in.

"Well. Thank you for sharing," said Ginny, breaking the ice.

"She doesn't mean that the way it sounded," Mrs. A quickly added.

"What do you mean? I did mean it. It's nothing new – her situation. She's very brave to tell us. But her 'situation' is nothing new. Maybe the how is different...."

Nancy laughed, "Nooo. 'The how' is always the same. Remember the sperm and the egg? The 'mommy and the daddy?' The penis and the vagina?"

"The double backed beast," Lisa chimed in. The other's wriggled awkwardly, not knowing if they should laugh or not.

"Enough!" Mrs. A cried, both her hands in the air to gesture stop. The smile on her face relaxed the group. "You're right, but there is always a story. Every woman has stories. Not all get caught this way, but Cheryl is 'caught.' She needs help figuring out her options."

Ginny added, "She needs help even after that. Options are great, but how do you get there after you decide, I mean, where do you go? How do you...."

"I get it!" Cate erupted.

Mia jumped, "Cathryn!"

Cate continued her attack. "Don't you think I know what's going on? I know what you're doing. You told them, didn't you Mother? You set me up! Couldn't keep it to yourself! Had to take over! You had no right! Like Grandma said, it's my story. I should have told her."

"Well.... Well.... I didn't.... I thought.... I'm sorry." Mia was wringing her hands as she concluded her apology.

Cate was sobbing and trying to disappear into the chair. Everyone was looking at her. Slowly the knowledge of Cate's situation filtered through to the three younger women. Cheryl was staring at her with awe. A little impatience ran across her face. Then her look hardened and she shut down again.

* * * * * * *

The worry on Mia's face was soon dispelled by the empathy of the group around her. Still, had she done the right thing by bringing her daughter here? Cate had demanded to "go to Grandma's." Mia had tried to convince her to deal with this within the family. "Grandma is family!" Cate had cried. She had brought up options for the young girl. The Good Shepherd's Home, cousin Jackie's. But no. Cate insisted on going to Grandma's.

Grandma wouldn't tell her anything different from her own mother, but Cate needed more. She needed to tell her Grandma A. She needed to feel loved as only her grandma loved her.

And Grandma moved swiftly to her. She knelt before her and pulled her body close. She stroked her head and cooed, "I love you, Cate. I love you." Her voice was low and calm. Not a whisper. But still not for anyone but Cate.

Cate sobbed and melted, and Cheryl stiffened and froze. Nancy and Lisa sat still, afraid to move and influence the scene around them. Mia looked at her daughter and her mother as if she were seeing two strangers. Two who were so close that there was no room for anyone in between.

"So," Ginny broke everything open. "We have two pregnant unmarried teenagers, who need help and advice. By the way, we guessed it before your mother said anything. It's really difficult to hide a pregnancy from two old women like your grandma and me. I think I'll make some tea. Anyone else?"

As she headed for the kitchen, the others jolted into life. "I'll help," came from Nancy.

"Sure," called Lisa.

"Nothing for me."

"Me either." Mia and Cheryl called.

Mrs. A and Cate remained in their embrace a few moments more. Then Mrs. A fumbled for tissues, one for Cate and one for herself. She stood up stiffly and sat on the chair arm, maintaining physical contact with Cate. She looked over at Cheryl until Cheryl looked up. Mrs. A smiled a small, gentle smile, until Cheryl glanced away, putting her chin in her hand and quickly wiping a tear away.

"I'll bring some for everyone," Ginny hollered. "Don't want to dehydrate with all this crying."

..*.*.*.*.*

"What kind of tea did you make? Pennyroyal? Blue Cohosh? Tansy?" Nancy asked when they came in with the tea.

"Earl Grey," Ginny answered. "Why?"

"We were talking about herbal abortifacients."

"Abortifacients?" Cate asked.

"Things that cause abortions, miscarriage," said Nancy. "I learned about them in my 'consciousness raising' group."

"'Group?'" Cate asked.

"Yeh. We get together to gripe and learn about 'sexism,' you know 'male chauvinist pigs' and such."

"Sounds interesting," Ginny said.

"Can you still get those herbs?" Lisa asked.

"Good question," Nancy answered. "They were pretty nasty and didn't always do the job. The doses were hard to control."

"What do you mean?" Cate asked.

"Well, contraception was not an exact science before the pill, you know."

"Yeh, Lisa's right." Nancy had a serious look on her face. "The rocks, sponges, shells and other things they put in the uterus weren't exactly clean. The procedure improved a lot, with information about sterilizing things becoming common knowledge. But women died. They tried different herbs, but some caused death or only killed the fetus and the mother still had to deliver the dead baby or worse, deformed the baby who then had to live with the deformity. Those were dangerous times. It really was a crap shoot."

Laughing, Lisa continued. "Some women thought if they did it standing up, they wouldn't get pregnant."

Nancy laughed too. "Some guys, and we all know some, said they'd pull out in time. Good luck!"

"Diaphragms and condoms were pretty good but messy," said Lisa.

Ginny said, "You know why women cry at weddings. In the past, fifty percent of brides would die as a result of pregnancy. Plenty of reason to cry."

..*.*.*.*.*

Everything had quieted down. The tea had been drunk. Casual conversations had begun and gone nowhere and died quickly. The women glanced at each other, but nobody engaged. Nancy and Lisa were making noises about leaving.

"So, I suppose it's time to head home. Sean probably has Rachel in bed already. Nice to see you, Ginny. And nice to meet you, Cheryl."

She started to get up when Cate asked Nancy, "Why do you guys laugh every time you say you're 'adopted.' I just don't see anything funny about that."

"That's one of those stories Mrs. A was talking about, right Nancy?" Lisa said.

"Right. My mom, Carol, Mrs. A's cousin, was head over heels for the farm boy next door. He didn't even know girls existed. This went on all through high school. All she wanted was to be a nurse and marry him and have his kids."

"He finally figured out what girls were for," Lisa laughed.

"Carol came to stay with me. She wanted to keep the baby and go to nursing school," Mrs. A added.

"But nursing school was residential back then," Nancy said.

"And so, Mrs. A took care of me."

"Just until your mom finished school. She came to see you whenever she could during her training. We were glad to have you here," Mrs. A continued.

"And my dad was really missing my mom. So, they finally got married and 'adopted' me," Nancy was smiling, almost laughing, as she finished the story.

"Why were they so sneaky?" Cheryl asked.

"Well, you know what people would think, don't you? 'By golly, they were doing it before they were married,'" Lisa scolded, playing the "old biddy.

"Not only that," Ginny couldn't help but add, "they didn't get married right away and have an 'early' baby. Everybody was counting on their fingers in those days."

"Yeh, right. They still count on their fingers," finished Nancy.

Cate responded, "It's better than jumping off a bridge like my grandma."

Cheryl looked at Mrs. A, shocked. "I thought you were her grandma."

Mia's voice broke in. "Let's not talk about this now."

"Why not, Mom? It's just the facts. It's Grandma's 'story.' We all know it. The whole town knows it. I'm surprised Cheryl doesn't already know it. Mrs. A and my grandma were sisters. Karen and Marion. When my grandma, Karen, jumped off the High Bridge, Mrs. A raised her kids, my mom and her two brothers. So, she became my grandma. I never knew the other one. Is there a 'normal' relationship in this whole family?"

"Cate!" chided her mom.

"Certainly not you and me!" Cate continued.

"Especially you and me!" Mia responded.

Lisa started to get up, but Nancy said. "In the old days, women took care of each other. A pregnant girl would move in with an aunt in another town and give the baby up. No one knew, so everyone was happy."

"There's the old story about a mom and her teenage daughter who went away on 'vacation,' and when they got back the mom had a new infant and the teenager had a new brother…or sister," Lisa added.

"Those were both better solutions than the hanger," countered Nancy.

"There were places to go," said Ginny.

"Gin, you don't have to…." Mrs. A almost whispered.

"Why not? It's the same old story. Tom and I weren't married, and we thought we'd 'fix it.' But everyplace we went was so awful. So dirty. One doctor told me I had a 'cyst', and he could remove it. I was too dumb to get his meaning. So, we came home and got married. Monday after our wedding, I was fired."

Lisa interrupted, "Wha…? Why?"

"A pregnant woman couldn't teach. The kids might suspect that we were 'doing it.' Tom was allowed to finish the year."

"What a bunch of crap," Cheryl muttered.

"That's the way it was," Ginny shrugged.

"But thank God for that darling little boy, Stevie! It worked out so well," Mrs. A said with a big smile.

"That's for sure. Anyway, eventually," smiled Ginny.

"Well, my grandma died!" Cate stated.

"A lot of women died," answered Ginny.

"Thank God for Margaret Sanger!" Nancy responded.

"Thank God for the pill!" Lisa shouted.

"Thank God for Roe v. Wade!" Ginny yelled.

"Let's not go that far," Mia muttered.

Cheryl looked over at her with intense interest. She had been listening closely to these family revelations. The pain of Cate and her grandma's death. The matter-of-factness of Nancy and Carol's stories. The jubilation of the "Thank God" chorus. And then it slammed suddenly shut with Mia's muttered caution.

..*.*.*.*.*

"What did they do in the olden days?" Cate asked.

"I heard they cut it off," Nancy answered.

"Really, Nans," Lisa snorted, laughing. "I heard they drank herbal teas for both prevention and abortion."

"That's why the tea party was so important! It wasn't just about gossip or fellowship. I'll be damned!" Cate seemed surprised at her own revelation.

"I told you they cared for each other," said Nancy. "They shared information. They helped with birthing, childcare, death. They taught each other what they needed to survive. I read they had a kind of code. They called it 'quickening.' You know, that 'leaping in the womb' thing. After feeling life, they went on with the pregnancy, or most of them did. Or they meant to. Over half of pregnant women died as a result of pregnancy. In childbirth. Or from exhaustion and complications from baby after baby."

"How do you know that?" Cate asked.

"We've read a lot. Women's journals, articles, books, 'MS' magazine. It's part of the new 'Women's History.' My group. We talk with our friends." Nancy was into it now. "Women know a lot, but they have to share. My mom said nobody told her anything. She thinks they thought if she knew about sex, she would do it. Well, she did it anyway. Nobody told her about labor. She was scared and unprepared and alone. She didn't know it would hurt or what would happen to her body. She told me, thank God, so I could know."

"She told you?" Cate looked from Nancy to her own mother. Her face was full of surprise and pain.

Mia looked hurt. Her response was full of care for her daughter. "I didn't want you to have to live with all that stuff. I thought, you know, in time. You always seemed so young. I wanted you to stay innocent."

"Yeah, innocent. Right," Cate muttered.

"No, really!" Mia exclaimed. "And you never seemed interested. You never asked."

"It doesn't matter, Mom."

"Well, we'll talk later, honey. Whatever you want. Whatever you need." She looked around at the group, turned and ran up the stairs.

"That was kind of tough," Nancy said.

"Let her go," Cate answered. "I need to know more about this stuff. Did you go to meetings? Are there books? Do we have a chance?"

..*.*.*.*.*

Lisa took up the conversation as Mia disappeared upstairs. "I went to a women's 'consciousness raising' meeting. The presenter said we need to know our bodies. She named the sex organs. And asked us if we had seen them. Well, of course, we had all seen boobs. And many had seen the male organs. She had those women describe them to the women who hadn't seen any. That was really funny."

"I bet some of the words were 'balls' and 'wiener,'" Ginny chuckled, and the others roared into laughter.

"That's pretty close," Lisa continued. "And when she named 'vulva,' 'clitoris,' 'vagina,' things got really interesting. Some admitted to seeing a vulva. I had no idea what it was, even though I had one. Many knew vagina but had not seen one. Very few admitted knowing clitoris. We were all very ignorant."

"Well, I wouldn't have done very well on that quiz. And I probably would've left about then," exclaimed Mrs. A. "I've never heard of that. Who sits around and talks about sex organs?"

"Guys," Nancy shouted. "And the size of them. And how, and who, and when."

"Not all guys," Lisa cut in.

"So, what did she do to 'enlighten' the group?" Nancy asked.

"She gave us hand mirrors to put on our chairs and have a look."

"Oh my God!" Ginny almost rolled off her chair laughing. "I can just picture it. What? Ten women crouched over their chairs looking at themselves. Or even, can you believe it? Touching themselves 'down there?'"

"What's so funny?" Cate asked. "I think it's really sad. When I got my period, I didn't know anything. Mom had given me some pads and a belt and said to ask if I needed anything else. She seemed so embarrassed, so I just ignored the whole thing and threw the stuff away. And then when it happened, I thought I was gonna die. You know, literally bleed to death. I went to Mom, and I didn't even know what to ask. She didn't get it. I finally showed her the bloody toilet paper I had stuffed into my underpants."

"You know, that's another set of stories. 'My First Period.' But maybe not right now," Ginny laughed. "So, did you do it, Nans? Look at your equipment in the mirror?"

"Not there! Oh my God! I would'a died first. But after I got home, I checked it all out. I mean I had felt those things, when I was masturbating, but I had no idea what they were called," Lisa said.

"I knew a girl who called her period 'Virginia.' I always thought she was talking about a weird friend," Nancy laughed.

"Well, I bet the guys have tons of names for the female organs. But none of those names," Ginny added.

"Pussy!"

"Bush!"

"Box!"
"Cunt!"
"How about 'breasts?'" Nancy called out.
"Boobs! Jugs!"
"Tits!"
"Knockers!"
"Rack!"
"Then there's 'woman.' Lisa added.
"Skirt."
"Squaw."
but 'woman.' Why can't we say 'woman?' Woman! Woman! Woman! Say it with me!"
"Woman! Woman! Woman!"
"There, I feel much better. How about you?"
"Enough! You girls are getting a little wild for us older 'broads,'" Ginny laughed and so did the rest of them. The energy in the room quieted with the realization of the words rocketing through the air.

"Well, it is almost the eighties after all. We need to all get with it." Lisa looked at her watch. "For Pete's sake, look at what time it is. Sean will be wondering what happened to us. And you must be exhausted," she said to Nancy. "We better head out. Cate, would you like some material to read? I have a lot of it."

"Yeah. Grandma has a lot of stuff upstairs, but I'd like to see more of the stuff you've been talking about. I feel really out of it, listening to you guys. Cheryl might like to read it too."

"Sure, my folks don't want me to learn anything but what they believe in and look where that got me," Cheryl looked amazed.

The four young women got up and hugged each other. Mrs. A led the way to the door and made sure her guests got in their car safely. She waved goodbye and turned off the porch light as they drove away.

Coming back, she saw Cheryl and Cate disappearing into the kitchen with the remains of the tea. Ginny was sitting there deep in thought.

..*.*.*.*.*.

"Quite a night," Mrs. A started.

Ginny looked up and sighed. "Life shouldn't be so hard."

"Now Ginny, that's not like you at all," Mrs. A stroked her friend's hair. 'You're always my upbeat."

"There's a reason I had all boys. God knew what I could deal with. Girls are a whole other thing."

The girls came back and said they had left the dishes in the sink if that was okay. Mrs. A answered, "Sure. Good night. Ginny and I will be right behind you."

The girls headed up the stairs. Ginny hefted herself off the couch and she and Mrs. A followed them.

Chapter 5

Mrs. A was in the kitchen, trying to come up with something for lunch. The dishes from last night were cleared away. Mia had slept on the couch and was upstairs in the shower. She had borrowed some underwear and a nighty. The girls were still sleeping, she thought. Good! Let them sleep in. They'd need it. Ginny had been down for a cup of coffee and had gone back up to her bedroom.

The refrigerator displayed pizza leftover from last night, a head of lettuce, celery, a quart of milk, eggs, and not much else. She knew she had some canned chicken, and if there was an onion, she could have chicken salad on lettuce and deviled eggs. Not a bad lunch. She found a can of black olives and a can of peanuts, and her lunch was organized. She assembled her ingredients and started the eggs cooking on the stove. A terrible sound shook her and the house. She fell to the ground as glass flew round her. A whooshing hot roar came through the smashed window.

Her ears hurt. Something ran down her face, into her eyes and mouth. When she touched her face, she realized it was blood. She pulled a shard of glass from the back of her hand and then another from her forearm. She stared as the blood rose in the now empty slits and also ran down in streams and puddled on the floor. She tried to get up. She rolled to her hands and knees and looked for something to grab onto and pull herself up. The heat above her drove her back to the floor. She saw the phone across the room with its cord hanging down the wall. She crawled across the floor. Glass crunched beneath her knees and hands. There was no pain really. And no sound. Funny. She thought she would never reach the phone.

Then something ran into her, knocking her to her side. She rolled, looked up to see Ginny grab the phone, dial, yell something. She watched as Ginny moved to the sink and turned on both faucets. She pulled down the burning curtains and doused them in the sink.

Mrs. A was fading. She heard noises, muffled and distant. She felt herself being moved. She saw things that didn't make sense. The last she remembered was her front door. She was moving through the opening on her back. She saw the angles of the door weirdly askew. She saw the sky. Clouds floated high. The sun was bright. A tornado of black smoke rose behind the house. And then she saw nothing.

..*.*.*.*.*

Mia was sitting. Her eyes peeking between the railings. Ginny was standing next to her, a smile spreading across her face.

"How are ya? Good to see ya," Ginny said.

"Mom?" Mia sobbed.

Ginny's hand went to Mia's shoulder and stayed there for a minute.

"What? Where? You? Are you all right?" she could barely hear their voices. One ear was ringing.

"Us?" Ginny answered. "We're great. The house is fine too."

"The house?" She was trying to remember, to put it all back together. Confusion. Images colliding in her mind. She looked at Mia. Her daughter stood up.

She breathed, "Mom, it…. We…. I'm so glad you're all right. How could they do this? What can they be thinking?"

"Mia, we're not sure. We don't know anything yet," Ginny interrupted.

"Know what?" The clouds were clearing and the memories from the kitchen were returning. She didn't like her memories, much less understand them. She shook her head, but they kept coming.

"What happened? What do you mean, the house? You all okay? Really okay?"

"Yes, Mom. It's only you and the back wall and the kitchen window. The firemen got it out right away. And you came here in the ambulance."

"Ambulance? Me? Ow!" She grunted as she tried to sit up and then fell back with a sigh. "But what happened? I remember I was on the floor. And the glass. And I was bleeding."

"They tried to…." Mia started only to be interrupted by Ginny again.

"The chief said it looked suspicious, that's all. They won't know anything for a while and they want to talk to you when you're up to it. But they'll wait. And until they have answers for us, we shouldn't jump the gun here." Ginny gave Mia a discouraging look, but it was ignored.

"Jump? They do this all the time. You can't stop them. They're insane! They think they're right. She has lived with it for years. And so have I. They think they have the right."

"Shoosh, honey. Really, I'm fine. More scared than hurt. What do the doctors say? Do I have to stay here?"

"They talk about blood loss and they stitched up your hand and arm. But it's mostly a matter of keeping the cuts clean. The nurse thought you could go home soon if someone is there for a day to watch you," Ginny explained.

"You and the girls will be around. But I should be okay. I feel stiff, but I remember falling. And you knocking me over, my dear klutz," she finished fondly. "Thank you, Ginny."

"Do you want to try standing, Mom?"

"Yeh, good idea. Look out though, I don't want to fall on you."

Ginny laughed, "That would hurt you more than us. Here we go."

Mrs. A scootched up to the edge of the bed. Reaching out to the other women, she eased down to feel the floor with her feet.

"There, we made it without a catastrophe," Ginny smiled. "Do you want to see the view here?"

Mrs. A looked up and laughed. Her window was packed full of a brick wall. But at least she could tell the sun was shining.

She started moving toward the chair by the window. The others hovered around her in case she would topple, and they might be needed. But she managed the transfer just fine. She looked at her hands and legs stretched out in front of her. Her one hand and her arm were bandaged. That must be where the stitches replaced the pieces of glass she remembered sticking amazingly out of her skin. She still had no real pains, just an overall achiness.

"I'd like to go home now. And Ginny, you have to get on your way."

"Not until we're sure you're okay and that someone will be able to take care of you. But you're right, the girls should be able to keep track of you. And you better let them."

"Really, Mom! You should just quit. Why keep doing this? Aren't you tired of it? Nobody likes us. Nobody comes to see you anymore. You never go out. I'm surprised you still answer your phone. I'm the only family still around. Why make life so terribly hard for yourself? Just stop!"

"Now, honey. How can I stop? How did I start? Somebody has to care. I care. They know it. I don't want a lot in life. But you're right. I am tired. It's different now, you know that. It's legal now. And you're doing okay now. Your own life. Your own home and family. And I do see you and my friends. Even some of the girls keep in touch. When they call, when they come, I just help. I just care." She covered her daughter's hands with her own. "Everything is changing now. And nothing is changing."

"That's part of the problem. So many people in and out all the time. I never know who's going to be there when I come. I wonder you can keep track of it all. Do you even know what's going on in your own house?" Mia chastised her mother.

Ginny interrupted. "Maybe this isn't the time for that discussion. We're all distressed by this and there really aren't any answers yet."

The nurse invaded the scene. Her briskness displayed her efficiency. She assembled Mrs. A's clothing and shoes and started to help her patient dress.

"You'll be out of here in no time. The doctor isn't prescribing anything. Aspirin, or whatever, should help with the pain. You might have some ringing in your ears for a couple days, but there's nothing permanent. When you see yourself, you might be shocked. But they're superficial wounds. There might still be some really small glass splinters in your hair. Try a comb over a sink. Be gentle. Any questions? Fine. I'll get your paperwork to sign." And she was gone.

The three women looked at each other and laughed at her bedside manner.

..*.*.*.*.*

When Mrs. A got home, she went straight to her kitchen. Her granddaughter was leaning against the sink, her back to the blackened empty window frame. She had a broom and dustpan in her hands, and a big smile spread over her face when she saw her grandma. The smile quickly became a frown when she saw the cuts on her face and the blood caked and dried in her hair and on her clothes. Cheryl had been facing Cate and swung around to see what Cate saw.

"Oh my God!"

"Really, is it that bad? I haven't looked yet. How are you two?"

"We're fine and our room is fine. The firemen are gone. We thought we'd clean up a little. Ginny, they said your room is off limits. Well, it's soaking wet in there and a lot of smoke got in there. We got your stuff out and hung it on the line."

Cheryl asked, "What the hell is going on? Those 'fire' guys said it was a 'Molotov cocktail.' Can you imagine? They took pictures and picked up some of the pieces before they left. They said they'd be back to talk with you. This is so weird. Does this stuff happen a lot?"

"Where's Mom?" Cate asked.

"She went right to her car. She said she was exhausted and needed a good rest at her house. I suppose. She not only slept on the couch last night, but she is really upset about this. Well, at least we're all fine. Nobody got hurt. The house can be fixed. Let me get cleaned up. And maybe I'll lie down a while myself."

"That's for sure, Marion. Let's go up now. We can comb your hair and you can take a shower. Maybe I'll join you on your bed since mine is 'soggy city.' You gals could come up with some ideas for dinner, okay?" Ginny helped Mrs. A out the door and up the stairs. She muttered something about "Probably hot dogs and mac and cheese."

On the way, they passed a mirror. Shocked, Mrs. A exclaimed, "For Pete's sake! Look at that! Good thing I had my glasses on, or it might have been bad." Her hands went up to her cheeks as she stared at her shredded face.

"What do ya mean? 'Might have?' You have the best skin I know. But now…?" Ginny's voice faded off.

"Oh no, don't worry. I heal well. And some more washing will help."

Ginny shook her head in happy disbelief. "Let's go, sunshine. We need our beauty rest."

..*.*.*.*.*

"Thanks for the weekend. It was great to see you again," Ginny gave her friend a strong hug. They were alone, saying their goodbyes.

As she hugged back, Mrs. A said, "Not much fun though."

"But very interesting, that's for sure. What next?"

"Well, as things settle down, we'll have to talk over possibilities and make arrangements for…. Well, for whatever."

"They're very different girls, uhh, women, I guess."

"Yeh, whether they're ready or not. They have women's issues to deal with."

They broke their embrace and Ginny picked up her bag and her purse. Hefting it to her shoulder, she headed toward the door.

"Here, let me get that for you." Mrs. A opened the door for her friend. "You know I'll miss you, right?"

"I'll be back soon. And you've got my number. Long distance is getting cheaper every day. Keep in touch. Let me know how this all turns out. I'm thinking I know what they'll do. But let me know. Not that I'm snooping. You know how I hate gossip."

"I know. We've never been into that. But, I'll let you know what I can. Give Tom a hug for me!"

"You too. Stay warm!"

"Don't even talk about it. Every year it gets harder to face the winter. But so far, this fall, it's been beautiful."

"Yeh, but. it is coming. Take care!"

"You too!" Mrs. A watched her friend go down the walk to her car. They waved again. Ginny climbed into her car after stowing her bag in the trunk. Mrs. A waved one more time as the car pulled away.

She looked around at the street. Her hand wandered over her cheek where the red cuts were scabbing over. All was quiet. The leaves were just starting to change color. Clouds were drifting high, and the sun was warm. Still, she shivered as she backed through the door and closed it with a click.

Chapter 6

The girls were in the backyard, throwing a football around. She recognized it. Bob and Randy used to play football with Al and sometimes Andrew. Cate had probably remembered that it was in the garage. Cheryl stumbled and fell in a pile of leaves. Cate immediately tagged her, and then fell down next to her. Their shrieking and laughter came to her through the open window where Mrs. A stood watching them. This is good, she thought, but we'll have to talk soon.

She looked at the blackened window frame and the mess around the sink. The Formica was scorched and would have to be replaced. She'd get something brighter, lighter, this time. New curtains too. What about the cupboards? This could get expensive. Should she call her insurance agent yet? Yeh. Shouldn't wait too long. It will be cold in the nights now and she would need the window fixed or boarded over. A quick call later would do. She needed the fire department's report and maybe she would learn something more about what happened. "Molotov cocktail indeed!" she said. Why did they think that?

She stepped outside to the backyard, waved at the girls still playing, tossing the football. She looked at the scorched wall by her kitchen window. Blistered paint spread out above a big black splotch on the cement patio. Her cushions and her wicker chairs were ruined. Would insurance pay for them? They were her grandma's, the wicker chairs at least. She had made the cushions herself. A couple plants had burned, but their pots would wash up.

The girls came over and stood beside her. They looked at the mess too. Cate said, "The fire chief said we could clean up outside. They took pictures both inside and outside, but they said another guy would come and inspect it. They said something about arson."

"Oh dear. After all these years, it's come to this, then," sighed Mrs. A.

"No, Grandma. Who would do this? Why would anyone do this?"

"There're plenty of people who would do this. My own parents would do this. They believe it's wrong, what you do. That you're a sinner. Even if you aren't a killer yourself, you help." Cheryl was almost livid.

"Don't talk like that! They're idiots! They can't decide for others! For sure they can't decide for me!" Cate stomped off into the house. Mrs. A put her arm around Cheryl and said, "She wasn't talking about your parents, Cheryl. She was just talking in general."

"But she's right. They not only want to decide for me, but for everyone. It's none of their business. They can believe it's a sin. They can believe it should be punished. But the law doesn't allow them to act on their belief, you know?" She looked up at Mrs. A. Her eyes were wide, but there was no anger or sadness. They were just steady and determined. They walked into the house together.

Chapter 7

"Grandma! Andrew's on the phone," Cate dashed out of the kitchen to find her grandma. Mrs. A came down the stairs and hurried to the phone.

"Hello sweetheart! How good to hear from you. Is everything okay? Becky and the kids? You? Oh, I'm out of breath, I was upstairs."

"What's going on Mom? What's all this I've been hearing about. Mia's practically hysterical. She called me late last night. Something about a fire? A bomb? What's the deal?" She knew the anger in his voice was because he cared about her. He was a lot like his dad. The first reaction was in defense of her. And this was usually expressed in anger.

"Oh, it was just a small fire. You know how Mia exaggerates. And we don't know what really happened. The fire chief hasn't been here yet."

"Why's the fire chief coming? That makes it sound even more serious."

"Not really. It could be arson, they think. But nobody got hurt. And the damage is just to the kitchen and the patio."

"Mia said you were in the hospital," Andrew's voice was calmer now. He was able to listen.

"Not for long. It was just scratches from broken glass. It looks worse than it is. Ginny was here."

"How long? Can she look out for you?"

"No, she's gone. But Cate's here."

"Oh, Mia didn't mention that. Funny. So, you're okay. Did you contact your insurance company? They have to see it before you start to fix it. Is it really cold up there now?"

"Not yet, but…."

"Oh, gotta go. Call me if you need me. Let Mia help you. I know how you two can get into it. But she's there for you if you need her. Keep me posted. Love ya, Mom."

"Love you too. Bye."

..*.*.*.*.

Her daughter Katherine had called earlier with much the same concern. She was also angry, but she had gone further than Andrew, blaming her mother's "activities" for the incident.

"You know this would never have happened if you'd just quit helping everyone who knocks on your door. Those radicals have got your number. They won't quit now until they get you. It probably isn't safe for you there anymore. Even if you never helped another girl, they won't forgive you for what you've done."

"You shouldn't listen to Mia, honey. She gets so carried away. And you know how she's always after me to give up and move in with her."

"Is that so bad, Mom? It would solve a lot of problems. You're not getting any younger. Or richer. And it's legal now. You don't need to do this anymore."

"I'm not that old, Katherine. And I'm holding on. I don't need rescuing yet."

"But obviously, you're in danger. Can't you see that? More than before when they tried to scare you with pig placentas in the bushes, blood splashed on the doorstep and all that other gross stuff. I never wanted to open the front door. I was always afraid of what would be there."

"I'm sorry about that, honey. Those times were awful. Well, we don't know anything for sure yet. I think I can wait a little and get the scoop before I make such a drastic decision. But I really appreciate your concern, Pumpkin. And I love you for it."

"I love you too, Mom. But I think you're being unrealistic about your situation. It's not about those 'awful times.' They bombed your house this time. I think you need to listen to Mia. She only wants to help."

"That's true. But I don't want to react to this by running away. Not that I'm that brave, but I think I still need to be here. Cate's here you know."

"Really," her daughter seemed surprised. "Mia didn't mention that. Well, you guys watch out."

"I'm always careful, you know," Mrs. A tried to sound convincing.

"Well, is the risk really worth it? I'm sorry. I don't mean to keep raggin' about it. I'll check back in a couple of days. Love you, bye."

..*.*.*.*.*

So, they had both made the obligatory contact. And they both knew what she would do. Or continue doing. They were good kids. She was very proud of them both.

As she expected, or was it hoped, Al called that night. She was sitting in the kitchen reading, just in case he would call. She didn't want the phone to wake the girls. And she was missing Ginny already.

Their's was a long friendship that didn't need a lot of maintenance, but each time they parted, she felt lonelier than before. Age. It was probably due to their ages. She continued in her reverie until the phone interrupted her. She jumped up, feeling the shock of the wounds and the arthritis, and moved as swiftly as she could to the phone. She got there on the third ring and settled down at the table for a long chat.

"You okay?" she heard a catch in his voice.

"Oh, yes, I'm alright. I take it you heard from Mia too."

"She called when I was out. Left a message with Shirley. Said it was urgent, so I called her right back. I can't talk long. Shirley's upstairs waiting for me. Do they know who did it?"

"No, but they have their suspicions. Ginny was here. Cate too."

"Not much fun for Ginny. How's she doing? I always loved that woman. So real. So solid."

"She's great. I'd sure like to visit her this January, February."

"You should, Marion. You should get away and enjoy yourself."

"I'll check into it. I'd really like to. How is Shirley?"

"Oh, she's swell. Feeling much better since the surgery. But wait! Did you say Cate was there? Mia didn't say anything about it."

"She's probably all caught up in this incident. You know how overexcited she can get."

"Not really. I always thought she had a handle on things."

Mrs. A wondered where this man had been all those years they were together. Sometimes she couldn't believe how he managed to distance himself from anything remotely troubling in their home. Whether it was the girls who came for help or their own kids.

"Have you and she visited lately?"

"Now Marion, don't go getting after me again. You know Shirley and I have been busy, what with her health issues and the cruise. What about Cate? She okay?"

"She just missed her grandma and came for a visit. It was too bad that she got messed up in this thing, but she was upstairs and wasn't hurt. She's been very helpful. I'm sure glad you called."

"Mia said 'suspicious.' What does that mean? Did they finally catch up with you? Pretty nasty business, if you ask me."

"We'll learn more later. I really don't want to think about it. And I'm surprised you want to talk about it."

"I don't really. I just wanted to make sure you're okay. I know nothing will ever change. But I do love you, and I don't want anything to happen to you."

"Thanks, dear. I miss you, but I'm glad you're happy now."

"Shirley's a great gal. She can think of so many things to do. We're so busy. I need a nap most days. Oh, she's calling me. I'd better go. You take care now. And be careful."

She hung up the phone and fought for peace. "So busy." Really. "Fun things." Fun things that cost money. Money he never spent with his first wife. He had certainly forgotten to mention the cruise before. She wouldn't give him the satisfaction of asking where they went on that cruise. And she should visit Ginny. But how was she supposed to pay for that? That was one of the longer conversations of their lives. Oh, forget it. Forget him. She was content. She would handle it. Five years on her own now. And really it was better. Really. Much of her feelings of guilt had left with him. He always made her feel like she wasn't doing enough for him and the family. He would never say anything, but she felt like he was always disapproving of her cooking, her cleaning, and her work with the girls. But that night Gretchen miscarried.... He had been so helpful then. He had helped get her into the car. And when she finally got home from the hospital, he had the blood all cleaned up and had soothed Mia and Katherine. They had heard the commotion and seen the girl standing in the hall with her bloody pajamas and watched their mom and dad help her into the car and their mom drive away into the dark night. She tried to learn what he had said, but his response was offhand. Her own talk with the girls seemed to calm them and to answer their questions. "Miscarriage." "Very early." "Baby couldn't make it outside." "Gretchen would be fine." "No, she'd probably go home now." "Yes, it was very scary."

Yes, her family had gone through so much over the years. Karen's death. Mia's crisis and therapy. Andrew's and Katherine's departures. "The girls" coming and going. Sometimes they were there for just a day, but often it would be months. And Al giving up on her. He needed more than she was willing to give. But when he left, he found a woman who gave him even less, and took much more. How could she have been so wrong about him? About what he needed? She wouldn't be critical about him and his response to what she needed. She realized she had never asked for much from him. And maybe he needed to be needed. And she didn't need him.

..*.*.*.*.*

But there was one other call. A real surprise. She fixed herself a cup of tea as she tried to get over Al's "idiocy." One sip, strong and determined. Her face was set, tight, her eyes narrowed. The next sip was cautious, her lips trembled and her eyes watered. Sip. Tight. Sip. Melting. Sip.

She caught it on the first ring. It was more a reaction followed by caution. Who would be calling now, this late? Her hello was timid and worried.

"That was a close one, Marion."

..*.*.*.*.*

"That was a close one, Marion."

The voice called up rich feelings. Inside her, the deep longing and the memories were overwhelming. She sat down at the table and held the phone with her two hands so he couldn't get away.

"You heard," she sighed. Warmth covered her body. Her pupils grew larger and tears started drifting slowly down her battered cheeks.

"I keep track, you know."

"Thanks, I really appreciate it."

"How are you?"

"Why, Dr. Keller, you do care. Sorry Ben. That was uncalled for," Mrs. A blushed at her audacious flirting. But she hoped it would hide the love that was drowning her at that moment.

"Always, Marion, you know that," he laughed back. "But how are you?"

"Sore. Confused. Perplexed. Yes, that's probably the best word. Perplexed."

"People are saying it's the radicals, you know the protestors. At least that's what I hear."

"Ben, please don't go that way. It won't help. Mia is all over that. She's got everybody seeing shadows."

"They're not shadows, Marion. I see them every day here at the clinic and when I drive to the hospital."

"Are you in trouble, dear?" Marion whispered.

"No. No. Nothing like that is going on. I just wanted to make sure you were okay."

"I'll be fine. I just have to find my direction again and maybe get a bodyguard. That's a joke, Ben."

"Yeh, funny. Are you going to stop?"

"That's what they want. Mia, Al, Kathrine, Andrew. But it's bigger than that. I have months when this isn't real in my life. And then a phone call or a girl at my door…. They just need help, you know. Even with the law changing. Not as often or as much as before. But I can still help."

"Yeh, I know. But if you weren't there…?

"But I am here. They know where I am. It's my home."

"You could move."

"I wouldn't get enough from the house. It's paid for and pretty reasonable, living here. Mia wants me to move in."

"How about that?"

"I'm not ready yet. That's a whole 'nother set of problems. I can't imagine. At least not now. How's your life?"

"Maddy's got cancer. She's not going to make it."

"Oh my God! How? Is she suffering much? How are the kids taking it?"

"Well, it broke them up pretty bad, but their lives go on. She doesn't seem to be hurting too much yet. It' a glioblastoma. Brain tumor. Not really treatable. Very quick. We tried surgery. Six to nine months. We're close to the end. I don't know how I'll.... You know how I feel about her. She's my life...." His voice broke. The silence lengthened.

Finally, she breathed, "I'm so sorry, Ben."

"She doesn't want to see the grandkids anymore. She sees people one at a time. But I don't think that will last much longer. I do love her. I always have."

"Yes, I know."

"Hey, I gotta go." His voice was raspy. She could feel the deep sadness. She wanted to hold him, console him. Feel his chest against hers again. Wrap her arms....

"Of course. I'm so glad to hear your voice again."

"Yeh, same here."

"I wish I could help."

"Yeh. No. It's gonna run its course. We'll get through it. It's so hard, you know. To see her like that. You take care. And stay out of trouble, damn it!"

She smiled at the expression. Just like him. "Mr. Tough Guy," she thought and chuckled to herself.

"I will," she whispered before the line went dead.

Now she could go to sleep. Now she knew someone really cared about her. She felt warm and safe. Yes, safe. In spite of the boarded-up window and the scorched cupboards and counter. She had her direction back. She was strong again. He didn't have to call. His life was certainly a mess now. So very sad. He had been so committed to his marriage, his family. His work. But he had taken the time to call. To connect with her again. She turned off the kitchen light and headed up the stairs to bed.

Chapter 8

She had been to the doctor for a follow-up on her cuts and to the grocery store for food. The girls had eaten everything she had and all that Ginny had stocked before she left. She came in with the bags of refrigerated and frozen items. As she opened the door, she heard the ripples of laughter and giggles coming from the living room. Cate and Cheryl sat on the tiny chairs, their knees rising above the little table. Mrs. A still hadn't restored the living room since the tea party with Rachel. They had found the tea set and had set the table. As she came through the door they jumped up.

"Is there more in the car?"

"We'll get it!" They rushed past her, still giggling.

They returned before she had even reached the kitchen and pushed through the door ahead of her, holding the door open with a foot until she could get through.

"Wha'd ya get?" Cheryl asked.

"Something good, I hope," Cate chimed. "God, I'm starving!"

"Hah! All four of us are starving!"

Cate looked puzzled at Cheryl's statement.

"Well, we're both eating for two, and two plus two is four."

Cate scowled and sharply turned her back to put items in the pantry.

"Sorry," Cheryl mumbled. "I guess you're not ready to talk about it."

Mrs. A moved to the edge of the conversation. Cate turned around and said, "I can't think about it yet."

Cheryl had postponed her appointment after the fire and was waiting to see what happened with Mrs. A. Cate hadn't opened up at all yet.

"Oh, the fire department called," Cate remembered. "Someone's coming around later to talk to you. Look! Cookies, cheese, crackers, grapes. Let's get our tea ready. Rachel will be here soon, right?"

Lisa had called and asked if Rachel could come over for the afternoon. She hadn't known about the fire. But Cate had assured her that Mrs. A was fine, the house was fine, and Rachel would be safe and they all would love to play with her.

"Right," answered Mrs. A. "I've got Earl Grey."

Cheryl's face wrinkled up. "Can I have juice instead?"

"No, silly," Cate responded. "It's a tea party. It'll do you good."

"Sounds like something your mother says a lot to make you do what you don't want to," countered Cheryl. Mrs. A chuckled at Cheryl's retort and Cate's discomfort. The chuckle changed the discomfort to laughter and they went about their chores.

They finished storing everything away and started preparing their tea. Mrs. A found the sugar cubes and poured a little milk into the little creamer. She poured the hot water over the tea leaves in the teapot, put them all on a tray and carried them into the living room. The girls brought in the "eats," and they all settled at the little table.

Sighs of comfort and companionship escaped the three.

"One lump or two? I'm sorry I don't have any lemon. Cream? I mean, milk? This is really nice," said Mrs. A.

"Maybe we should wait for Rachel?" Cheryl asked.

"You're right, Cheryl," Mrs. A said thoughtfully. "It would be rude to start without our little guest. She'll bring her little Koala Bear, I'm sure. She is so much fun."

"I remember all those tea parties we had, Grandma. It's been so long. I used to bring my stuffed dog. And one time I brought an imaginary friend, but you were so great about it. You pretended right along with me. It's been so long. I'm sorry. I've missed them."

"I've missed them too. But it's good to be all grown up, right?" Mrs. A asked.

"No!" Cheryl answered looking at the teacup in her hand.

"Not in my case anyway," Cate added. "Besides, I don't feel grown up. I feel like a kid. I play ball. I watch TV. I read books. I don't have a job. My mom wants me to clean my room and help around the house. I'd rather go shopping or bum around. I don't know anything. I'm scared. How did this happen to me?" She covered her face with her hands.

"Boy, for somebody who can't think about it yet, you're sure thinking about it," Cheryl muttered.

"Well, it is the reason we're here together in this room," Mrs. A responded. "It is something we have to look at soon. But there's a lot to it. Cheryl, you're absolutely right. You're not adults, but you have an adult problem. How would you like to see this go? How do you picture yourself?"

"Not in some dirty apartment with a dirty baby crying and me too. I don't know how to clean, cook, pay bills. I've never worked, for God's sake. My folks give me an allowance. I don't save anything. This is so stupid!"

Cate spoke softly. "I can see me with a baby. I mean, my mom has said I can stay home. She'll support us until I'm out of college. She'll help with the childcare, it would be okay. But still. I don't want the baby. But it isn't the baby's fault. I have nightmares. I can't go anywhere. I'm afraid all the time. I can't look anyone in the face. I can't.... I.... I hate this."

They all jumped when the doorbell chimed. Mrs. A rose to answer. She left the girls glum and staring at each other.

"We can't carry on in front of Rachel, you know," Cheryl whispered.

"Yeah, but I guess we better talk.... Later," answered Cate.

Rachel came shyly into the room dragging her Koala bear with one hand and holding Mrs. A's hand with the other. Her hat sat back on her curls and her eyes were big and deep. The girls started to get up, but when Rachel hid behind Mrs. A, they quickly sat down again. Rachel peeked at them and they smiled and giggled.

"Rachel, you know my granddaughter, Cate. And this is my new friend Cheryl."

Cheryl looked at Mrs. A, surprise turning to appreciation.

"I have a friend too, my Koly." She held her bear high and asked, "I'll put him in his highchair?"

Mrs. A said, "Rachel's Mom had some errands. She said you two said it would be okay. She wants to see the damage when she comes back. Maybe we can talk her into staying for supper."

"Where's your hats?" Rachel asked. Cate and Cheryl looked about.

"Let's see what I can find," answered Mrs. A.

She went into the other room and they heard her opening doors and drawers. "Go ahead, I'll just be a minute. Rachel, one lump or two?"

"Two please. Oh, grapes. I love grapes. Koly, would you like some cheese and crackers?"

The three were busy serving each other and Koly when Mrs. A came back, a long filmy scarf wrapped around her head with the ends hanging romantically near her face. She had the big hat from the other tea party and a smaller hat in deep red with a narrow brim and a big button on the ribbon band. "You two will have to figure out who gets which."

"Cheryl's long blond hair will look great in the big hat. Hey, that's the same hat from when I was little!" Cate noticed.

"And you'll look terrific in that red," Cheryl added.

Hats on their heads, they continued their tea in earnest. Chatting. Laughing. Stirring. Clinking. Pinkies in the air. The two older girls were leading the fun. Mrs. A observed quietly. Smiles broke regularly across her face. Laughter bubbled up freely.

The doorbell rang again. “It’s too early for Mommy,” Mrs. A said. She got up to answer the door.

“Maybe it’s the fire chief?” guessed Cate. She started to wipe Koly’s face. “That’s enough for you, my fine furry friend.”

“He’s not your friend, he’s mine. I can do it.” The pout on Rachel’s face was more a demand as she snatched the napkin Cate held ready to clean the bear.

“Sure.” And Cate relinquished the wiper to the small one who attacked the bear as if he really was dirty.

”Good work! Do you want to help with the dishes?” Cate asked. “We can take them into the kitchen, and you can wash them. We have a stool you can stand on. Do we have an apron, Cate?”

Rachel’s face brightened and she grabbed her little plate. “I can carry my own dish. Mommy let’s me help at home.”

The girls gathered up the rest. What didn’t fit on the tray, Cate stacked up to carry. She almost dropped them all as Rachel turned about and roared past her. “Koly! You come help too!” She grabbed her bear and raced back to the kitchen.

“Look out below!” Cheryl yelled. “Girl and bear on the loose. Roly poly Koly Bear, beware! Beware!” she sang.

“Where be bear, take care! Take care!” chanted Cate back. “Berry bear with no hair. Bare Bear! Bare Bear!”

"Berry berry! Bear! Bear! Bear!" added Rachel enthusiastically.

Chapter 9

Mrs. A could be heard talking with a man. They heard the two of them going upstairs. They were walking around the rooms upstairs. Doors opened and shut. Windows went down and back up. They had left the two bedrooms opened to get the smoke smell out and to help with drying everything. The fire had been put out quickly, so everything would return to normal soon. Well, the house would anyway, return to normal that is.

They were coming back down now. All three girls were watching them.

"This is Chief Douglas," Mrs. A introduced the man with her. "This is Cate Mayer and Cheryl.. uh, Smith. And Rachel," she smiled as she said the child's name.

He nodded at them. "Were you both here the other day?" the Chief asked. He had a clipboard and was writing. Their names probably. Cheryl looked a little concerned at what he might be writing.

"Yeah, we were upstairs," Cate answered.

"Together?" the Chief asked.

"Uh," Cate looked at Cheryl, a little panic came and left her face again.

"No," Cheryl answered. "I was in the bathroom across the hall."

"And I was asleep. The noise woke me up," Cate added.

Chief Douglas wrote down something. Lifting up a page on his clipboard, he puzzled over something he was reading. "Your friend,

'Virginia,' said she saw Cheryl coming out of the office and Cate standing in the bathroom door"

"Well, ya," Cate stuttered. "I ran in there to see what happened."

"And I went into the office to get a better look. I couldn't believe it. The fire spread so fast, it looked like an explosion."

"Virginia called in the alarm, right?" the chief asked.

"Yes. When we came downstairs, she was trying to drag Grandma into the living room. So we helped her."

"She said she had called for help." Cheryl added. "She said to get out of the house."

"Then we heard the sirens. And the firemen helped us. They carried Grandma out and into the ambulance. It really happened quick. What is going on?"

"Well now, that's what we're going to find out." The chief looked up from his clipboard and asked Cheryl. "So your name is Smith?"

"No." Cheryl looked at Mrs. A. "I didn't tell her my last name. And she didn't ask."

"I suppose she calls all her girls Smith or Jones. But, young lady, I need to know your real name. For the report, you know."

"Can I write it for you? And can you keep it private?"

"Well, it is an official report. How old are you?"

"Fifteen."

"So, you're a minor. We don't publish the names of minors. What about your parents?"

"I called them. They said I should stay with Mrs. A. If she needed me, that is."

Cate and Mrs. A both looked at her in surprise. Neither one had seen her on the phone. But then they didn't keep track of each other every minute. And it had been rather chaotic. And they thought she was older, but neither one of them could remember if they really knew or not. But she had made that call to the clinic, didn't she say she was eighteen?

Chief Douglas took some measurements and wrote and drew pictures of the damage. He noted how far the flames had burned. "And where were you standing, Mrs. Anderson?" He wrote down her answer. "Did you get burned, or splashed with liquid?"

"No," Mrs. A answered. "Just cut by flying glass."

"I see that's all been cleaned up. But can you show me about how far it flew? Where most of it was?"

She gestured and described the scene. "I was standing here. And then I was on the ground. There was glass everywhere. But not by the phone."

"That's true," Cate said. "I swept up, but there wasn't any glass there."

"Not on the counter next to the door either. It was mostly over there, in the sink and on the counter next to the sink."

"There's no scorching there either, I see. Only next to the sink," the chief added. "Well, let's go outside and see the rest of the damage."

Mrs. A suggested Rachel take her bear into the living room and read him a book. "I won't be long and then we can have a little nap."

Outside they found more scorched areas mostly on the one side of the window and on the patio area.

"Did you clean up here too?" the chief asked.

"Well, the chairs were all over and burned and chipped," Cate answered.

"The cushions were ruined," Mrs. A added. "They're still behind the garage if you want to see them."

"Yes," the chief nodded. Then he stooped and picked up a piece of glass left under a bush. "Doesn't look much like window glass. Where did you say you put the glass you swept up?"

"In the garbage can. That's behind the garage too." Cate and the chief headed behind the garage.

Cheryl looked hard at Mrs. A. She seemed scared, but defiant.

"It's okay, Cheryl. I'm glad you talked with your parents. They were sure to hear something or read it in the paper. I'm sorry for the delay. We do have to talk and plan. Maybe tonight? The three of us?"

The Chief and Cate returned. He closed the cover of his clipboard. "I'll write a report and send you a copy." He held a plastic bag with pieces of glass. "You see, there's two kinds of glass here. This is the window glass, but this is bottle glass. This piece of cushion here, smells like gasoline. That and the scorching path tell me that we have a deliberate fire here."

All three women were stunned. "Arson?" Mrs. A gasped.

"Worse," the Chief answered. "More like an attack. You know, a homemade incendiary device."

"Molotov cocktail! Mom was right!" Cate was shouting, she was so scared. "Did they really dare do it?"

"They who?" the Chief asked. He looked at each of them expectantly.

"I don't know. Those people. You know," Cate answered.

"No, I don't. But it doesn't matter, because this device was thrown from inside the house. Probably that window up there." He pointed at the office window. Everyone looked up to that window and then down to the house, the patio and the kitchen window.

"You see," the Chief continued, "the device, surely a bottle, hit here on the patio and exploded. The forward motion of the bottle caused the flammable liquid to splash in that direction." He waved his arm to indicate the scorch marks. "The glass in the wall outside here is bottle glass, different from the window glass inside. I even know the ignition material, but that'll need more testing and verification. But, it'll be in my report." He held up a bag containing something charred and unrecognizable.

"Well, I have your statements and this evidence. I'll be sending a report to the police also. I'm sure they'll be contacting you. Your insurance company can get a report from them too. And you can get someone to assess the damage and board up the window. It's gonna be getting cold any day now. Any questions?"

The three stood in silence, each thinking about the Chief's statement, "from inside the house," which had shaken their world.

"Then, if something comes up, call me. Thanks for your time." He walked away, around the corner, and he was gone.

Mrs. A stumbled into the house. The girls watched her. Slowly, they turned to each other. Cate hugged herself and shivered. She looked to Cheryl, she said, "Who?" Cheryl slowly shrugged her shoulders and whispered, "At least we know why." They followed Mrs. A.

..*.*.*.*.*

"You said 'we know why.' I sure don't. Who would throw something like that? Maybe one of those radicals. But he said 'inside the house.' That's one of us." Cate was breathless and frantic. "Not them."

"It's okay," Mrs. A said in a soothing voice.

"It's not okay!" Cate shouted. "There are only four people it could be! Me! Cheryl!" She pointed at herself and then at Cheryl across the room, "Mom! Or Ginny! You couldn't have done it, you were in it."

"I can't deal with it now," Mrs. A responded. "Rachel is here. I'm going to wait for that report. I think we have to go on. We have to deal with your issues. After I rest a little and Rachel has her nap. This is beyond comprehension. Beyond me. I can't even imagine. It looks like what he said is true, but he could be wrong. I mean, how could it be? Rachel, honey, come along with me. I really need a nap and Koly looks like he needs one too. We'll just rest a bit. You girls, I mean it. Until we find out more, I don't want to hear anymore about it.

It's just too upsetting." She made her way up the stairs for their nap, holding Rachel's hand.

Cheryl and Cate stared at each other. Cate shook with the anger she couldn't suppress. Cheryl's hands were behind her, her expression unreadable. Her head leaned to one side and her eyes moved away from Cate's onto a distant space. "Why would any of us do that?" she asked. She turned and followed Mrs. A upstairs.

Chapter 10

Cate crashed out the front door, a resounding "Shit!" followed by a slam and she was gone. She started out walking, but quickly began running. Not a jog. Not even a sprint. But a full out passionate race with whatever thoughts she wanted to beat. She ran hard. If a car or a stoplight or anything got in her way, she simply turned and ran on in a different direction.

She was on a very shady street. The tree roots had lifted up chunks of sidewalk. She stumbled at one of the cracks. Arms swinging wildly, she regained her balance, stood there trembling, fighting her way back to reality. She glared at the street and houses. Panting, she sat on a stone wall. Her hands slid down her legs and grabbed her toes. She stretched, her breathing heavy. The movement was not as easy as it had been a couple of weeks ago. She almost could not reach her toes. She tried to press her head against her knees and let out another "Shit!" A quiet "shit" this time as her body reminded her of her situation. In that soft expression was an ending to her anger. A resignation to an inevitability.

"Just the four of us. "Not them. One of us. Cheryl? Ginny? Mom? Who?"

With that thought, she finally looked around and realized she had no idea where she was. "Stupid!" she yelled at herself. Still panting, she looked up the street. She was in the middle of the block. On one end she could see the sun shining down. She walked to that corner and looking at her watch, she figured out which way was west. She looked at the street signs. No help there. She didn't recognize either name. Her grandma lived on two numbered streets. And southwest. If she could find some streets with numbers instead of words, she could maybe figure out which way to go.

She wasn't really tired, but she was thirsty. A few blocks to the west, she saw lots of cars crossing the intersection. For now, the Fire Chief and his implication were pushed down. She started jogging toward the busy intersection, noting street signs as she went.

The busy street was also a name. Not far along the road was a gas station and possibly help.

..*.*.*.*.*

She came out of the gas station, piece of paper in one hand and paper cup in the other. She gulped the cup of water and turned to her left. She gave a thankful gesture toward the station window and threw her cup in the garbage can before jogging off.

With all her twists and turns in her mad run from Mrs. A's house, she had ended up only two miles away. Within half an hour she was entering the house. She could smell the cooking from the kitchen, but dashed up the stairs before they could catch her. She wanted to wash up and change before she encountered Mrs. A and Cheryl. She didn't have time to call her mother before Cheryl appeared at the door. As she pulled on her pants and looked up and saw Cheryl standing in the doorway looking at her belly. She quickly zipped her pants, not an easy task anymore. She pulled her shirt on and said, "What's up?" to the girl who she had thought would become a friend.

"Dinner's ready. But you don't have to hurry."

"No, I'm ready. And I'm starving." She couldn't help being friendly. They had so much in common.

"Your grandma couldn't sleep, so she came down right after you left. She said she wouldn't talk about it until after she had the report. And that was final. So be careful. She's really upset. You must be too, to run off like that. You were gone almost three hours. Mrs. A was really worried."

"Got it." They started down the stairs, Cate leading the way. Cheryl paused and put a hand on her own flat belly before she followed.

..*.*.*.*.*

Rachel's mother had come to get her and had been given a tour of the damage. She decided not to stay for dinner and add to the stress.

The meal was good, if anyone noticed. The girls filled their plates twice, but Mrs. A just pushed her food around her plate. She was the first to take her plate over to the sink. She scraped the plate clean and stacked it next to the sink. She turned around and Cheryl was standing there with her plate. Cate stepped up behind her. They both stood looking at their empty plates.

"I'm taking my coffee out to the patio. Would you both join me?"

"Sure, after we do the dishes," Cate answered.

"Yeah," Cheryl added, reaching for the towel as Cate started the water running into the sink. "Pretty serious sounding," she whispered as Mrs. A left.

"Shhh!" Cate whispered back.

..*.*.*.*.*

They finished the dishes and wiped up the counters and table. Cate reached into the refrigerator and brought out the orange juice. "Want some?"

"Uh huh," Cheryl said. She got out the glasses. "Some ice too?"

They went out to the patio with their iced juice. Mrs. A had arranged what was left of the furniture in the unscorched part of the patio. She had her feet up on one of the chairs. As the girls joined her, she dropped her feet and smiled up at them. Such a tired smile.

"Regardless of all this," she waved her hands to indicate the patio and the house, "We have to talk about you. Every day, your options are changing. I'm sure your thoughts are changing also."

"Not really," Cate growled.

"Well, what can I help you with?" The two girls were silent. "Where do you want to start?" Still silence. "Cheryl, I know a little bit about you and the circumstances. Would you like to reschedule your appointment at the clinic?"

"The one on Central?" Cate asked.

"Yes, that's really the only option now," Mrs. A answered. "But they're very accommodating."

"Yeah, I got my birth control pills from them," Cheryl said. In response to their surprised looks, she continued. "I know, how'd I get here if I had the pill? Well, my mom found 'em. In my drawer! After a lot of yelling and screaming and crying, she took 'em. She said she wouldn't tell my dad, because it would kill him. Or maybe he'd kill me. She didn't know which. So, I was screwed. I mean…." She blushed and turned away.

Cate snorted a laugh and said, "Yeh, really."

Mrs. A waved her hand in dismissal. "I'm glad you two still have a sense of humor. That's always helpful. Do you know the place, Cate? Would you like to go along when we go, or would you like your own appointment?"

"No, maybe it's easier if we go together, for us and for you, Grandma. Do they allow that?"

"Probably, but at some point, you'll get private counseling. Your mom won't have to be there, Cate. You're not a minor. But Cheryl, you must have a file from before. Did you tell them your name?"

"Yeh, for the prescription. You're right. Do you want me to make the call?"

"Yes. Early tomorrow. I don't know when you can get the appointments, but I don't think you should let them delay you."

"Yeh, Cate's starting to show. How far along are you?" she asked the other girl.

"None of your…." She stopped herself. "Sorry, I've been alone with this so long. I didn't mean…."

"Do you know?" Cheryl asked.

"What the hell kind of question is that? I'm not…. I mean, I don't…."

"Neither do I!" Cheryl laughed. "But I guess it doesn't matter."

"To me it does!" Cate cried. She was trying to keep the tears and the anger down. Mrs. A reached over and enfolded her hand. She squeezed gently and the young woman began to relax.

"I'm not putting you down. I only mean we ended up in the same situation. At least you seem to have your parents on your side, or at least your mom. And Mrs. A is your grandma. And she's on your side for sure. I'm not whining here. We were going steady. I thought it was 'love.' Crap! I got the pill. I planned how to 'give' myself to him. What a sap! And when it finally happened, everything ended. Oh, not right away. He enjoyed it too much. But that's all it was, S.E.X. He had no other use for me. We didn't go to movies or hang out with friends. Just sex. I invited him over for stuff, but if we didn't have sex, he'd just leave. So, I decided to stop the sex. When he finally got the message, he was gone. He's such a jerk! And I'm so stupid!"

While she was speaking, she had been looking at the wash line. When she finished, she turned her gaze to the other two. "So, that's my story. Now you know."

Mrs. A was looking at her with care. Cate was looking at her feet. "Asshole," she muttered.

"I'm glad you could tell it, Cheryl. He really is a 'jerk,' but not that different from many boys. And you can call yourself 'stupid,' but that doesn't help now. What do you want to do?"

"I'm not having it! I need to take care of it without my family knowing anything. I want to go to college, get a good job. I don't want this dragging me down the rest of my life. Girls like us end up poor. Their kids get a rotten start. Without friends and support, there's not much to do. You can't even work and you sit in your cheap apartment waiting for your government check. You can't afford to do anything or go anywhere."

"There's gotta be more to it," whispered Cate.

"Sure, you have the baby to play with, but that's the only positive I can see. And the baby isn't a doll. It cries, spits up, shits, and as far as I can tell, the mother is a slave to the little twerp."

"I won't let you talk like that. None of this is the baby's fault. You're right about what a baby is and does. But there is so much more," said Mrs. A.

"You mean not getting any sleep or a moment to yourself to even take a bath?"

"Cheryl, I can see that you have spent a lot of time trying to rationalize your decision. And I'm not here to change your mind. But there is something between the mom and the baby that no one can understand until it happens. This makes a lot of the work bearable. It's something you have to take on faith. Think about the women in your life who have had babies. Very few of them regret it. No matter how difficult. But I'm glad you're thinking about it, because these are every new mother's thoughts, no matter how good the situation or the support is."

"But Mrs. A, a baby is a lifetime. Where's my life?"

"That's why there is a choice. It is your life. Your decision. Not mine, not your parents' either. But I'm glad you're listening and thinking. The counselors should bring up a lot of issues. And they're there to answer your questions. Tonight, I would like you to write out all your questions. Not just about this pregnancy, but about your future.

You said a baby is a lifetime. But right now, in this situation, 'no baby' is a lifetime too. This is the most important decision of your life, so far. You have to be sure you can live with what you decide."

"Grandma." Cate almost choked. "I thought you would just take us to get it done. You know, make the appointment and everything."

"I will if that's what you want. I'm sorry. I'm confusing and upsetting you. But I want you to consider this now and not after it can't be undone. Make your decision from serious thinking, not fear or anger or disgust."

"Are you suggesting adoption?"

"No!" Cheryl jumped up. "No, they'd have to know then. I couldn't do that alone. Everyone would know."

"You could go away. And you can go to college without your parents' help. I've heard of kids doing that." Cate was trying to be helpful.

"Cate, do you hear what you're saying? I need to finish high school. Get into a college. If I go away, I can't do that. My folks would have to know. They'd disown me. Throw me out."

Mrs. A interrupted, "Really, Cheryl. Aren't you being over dramatic?"

"No! You don't know them. I've listened to them all my life. I know how they feel. I'm dirty. My dad calls girls like me names. He'd be disgusted. My mom would cry. I'd be a failure. I am a failure. I'm so stupid." Her tears overwhelmed her and she sagged back into her chair.

They all sat in silence. The sun was going down. Mrs. A looked at her watch. It was only eight o'clock, but the fall evenings were getting shorter and cooler. She shivered a little, but sat still, waiting for the next act of the play to start. These discussions were like improvisations. The same subject, but each actor's expressions were unique, her own. It was unusual to have two girls with her at once. And she never imagined having her own granddaughter caught in this life net. But here they were. She waited.

..*.*.*.*.*

"What is 'quickening?'" Cate asked suddenly.

"What?" Mrs. A struggled to change her thoughts. "Quickening?"

"Remember, Lisa and Nancy talked about in the old days and 'quickening.' The women would keep the baby after 'quickening'. What is that? Why would that change their minds or relieve their stress?"

"That's when the baby kicks you, right, Mrs. A?"

"Well, it's even before that. It's the first movements of life that a mother feels."

"Like when?" Cate's eyes were big in the dusky light and glossy with tears close to the surface.

"Oh, probably about three -- four months."

"What's it feel like?"

"It's a fluttering. It's so delicate, you almost miss it. You think it could be a gas bubble. You don't necessarily show on the outside yet. Although some women do. But it keeps up. And gets stronger. My babies did gymnastics every night. They'd start as soon as I'd lie down. It made it hard to sleep. But it was fun to try to figure out what was an arm, a hand, a head. Al and I used to laugh. He'd put his hand on my stomach to feel it. He'd always exaggerate the kick with his hand flying way up. I think he was really scared when it happened. But, 'quickening' is a private communication between mother and baby. Saying 'I'm here.' It's amazing." Mrs. A was watching Cate as she answered the question. Cate had tear streaks on her cheeks that were silver from the moonlight that had followed the dusk during their time on the patio.

"Have you felt it, Cate?" Cheryl asked, a scared look on her face.

"For God's sake, what difference would it make? Nobody can stop you if you really want to get rid of it. Right Grandma?"

"Right. Sort of," Mrs. A answered.

"What do you mean? 'Sort of?'" Cate looked really scared.

"They will go over the rules at the clinic, Cate."

"No, Grandma, really, how can they stop you?"

"Well, age is an issue. Some girls need their mom and dad's permission. And if they can't get that, they may have to go to court. That take's time. Then there's the counseling requirement. They don't want you making snap decisions. So, they schedule another appointment. The first appointment is to inform you and the law requires them to tell you certain things. They make you come back again for the procedure. These rules are part of the compromise. The anti-abortion people hope that with these delays, a woman will change her mind."

"Right, like she hasn't been thinking about it every minute," Cheryl laughed. She jumped up indignantly. Turning around like a cat looking for a comfortable spot, she settled into the chair again. "I mean…really!"

"And these things are laws? I thought things had changed. Grandma, some women would change their minds. And maybe it wouldn't be right. I mean, not the right thing."

"Well, and some women might change their minds, and maybe it would be right. You have to deal with the system as it is now. I thank God that things have changed, at least as much as they have," said Mrs. A.

"But some women might still…. You know, do something awful. And if you're too young, especially. I mean…. My grandma must have been really desperate."

"She probably couldn't see any way out. She couldn't go home with the baby, she couldn't go on without the baby. She had no way to make it on her own, with four kids. Although, if she had come to me, we could have worked something out. I could have watched her kids too. I was home with mine anyway. We could have managed. I didn't know she was going to do it. She was so troubled, so alone. I can't imagine the terror that would make her do that. I went there. I saw it. How she had to climb up and over. And then where she landed. So far down below. I guess a lot of people use that bridge that way. I can't understand how they can do it. But I can do what I do. Maybe somebody…."

"I don't know, Grandma. She must have known how much you loved her. But maybe that wasn't enough."

"But she left her kids didn't she. How could she do that? If she wanted them so much, how could she do that and leave them with their dad?" Cheryl was both angry and upset.

"Maybe she just couldn't imagine life anymore, but she knew that Grandma would be there for her kids. Maybe she was just falling apart inside. Maybe she thought she was no good."

"Are we talking about my sister or you Cate? Is this how you feel?" Mrs. A was looking at her. Her concern was strong and wary.

"Grandma, I didn't do anything wrong. Really. Please believe me. I don't want to do anything wrong. But what is right? I have more options than Cheryl. Well, I do, Cheryl. You're afraid of your parents. My mom says she'll help me."

"What about your Dad?" Cheryl asked. "You never talk about him."

"I told my mom not to tell him. I just couldn't stand it if he knew. I'm his 'little princess.'"

"But, this has already changed you, honey, don't you think he's noticed?" Mrs. A asked.

"Oh please, he's a man. Notice? Hah!" Cheryl cut in.

"He loves me and I don't want to hurt him."

"You should have thought of that before you did it."

"Damn it, Cheryl! You don't know anything. I didn't do it."

"Oh, the second virgin birth. That's it?"

"Shut her up, Grandma."

Mrs. A stood up. "I asked you to write down your questions and issues. Maybe this discussion has got you thinking. So, you can go inside and write. Do you think you can work at the same table or do you need to be separated?" The girls glared at each other. "You're in the same boat. How or why is your business. I'll be in the living room. I have a good book going. There are two tables, the kitchen and the dining room. There's paper in the little desk in the dining room. Pencils should be in there too. Help yourself to drinks and snacks, but get to it." She smiled and left them standing there in the dark.

"Well," Cheryl said, "who would'a guessed there would be homework?"

"She sure is something. I'm confused. I'm scared. But I feel safe here with her," Cate answered.

"Me too.' Cheryl paused. "Do you think there's any ice cream lcft?"

..*.*.*.*.*.

Mrs. A could hear them rummaging around the kitchen and the freezer opening and closing. She heard dishes clattering along with silver and the freezer refrain again. They rushed through the door and deposited their snacks on the dining room table. Cate opened the desk drawers and gathered paper and pens. She handed them to Cheryl who divided the paper into two stacks. "Red or black?" she asked holding up two pens.

"Color or ink?" Cate shot back.

"Color."

"Black, suits the subject better."

"So does red. Maybe better than black even," Cheryl commented.

They settled down to their assignment. Mrs. A could hear big sighs, grunts, quiet "damns" and "hells" from the adjoining room. She put her feet up on the hassock and lost herself in her book.

* * * * * * *

"Grandma, why can't you just answer our questions?" Cate complained from the dining room.

"I could, but you have to figure out the questions first. You'll probably have plenty more after tomorrow. But these people at the clinic are experts. On the law and on feelings. They've been doing it for a long time." They were talking across the rooms, but nobody gave up their position even if they were yelling a little.

"But Mrs. A, you've got experience and you know so many girls who …?"

"Yes, I do, Cheryl. But you have to go through the ritual tomorrow and I want you to make good use of the appointment. I don't think you should argue with these people. Just get answers to your questions and bring up anything you need to. Even if you think you know the answer or that you've made up your mind. You have to do this by law. But it doesn't have to be a waste of time."

"But they're just going to go over the same old stuff. Grandma, I don't want to change my mind, but they're going to press me."

"If there is any pressure, it will probably be coming from inside you. Their job is to give you information to help you make your decision. They can't force you into anything. One way or the other. They shouldn't argue with you, and you don't have to argue with them. Ask your questions and listen respectfully. It's their job. But it's your choice."

"Some choice," Cheryl snorted. "Have it, don't have it, put it up for adoption, keep it. Oh, ya, marry the bastard."

"I don't even know...," Cate whispered. She put her head down on the table and sobbed.

Mrs. A was up and beside her in a breath. She pulled a chair close to her and whispered, "Are you ready yet?"

Cheryl looked on with wide eyes.

"It was prom," she choked.

"Jay?"

"No! Grandma, no. Not Jay. He would never... No, he's my friend. Oh, God!" The sobbing continued, but more softly. "He doesn't even know. We were talking about the prom in the car. And you know, kissing and well...he fell asleep."

Cheryl started laughing. "Some kisser you must be."

"Cheryl!" Mrs. A said, chuckling herself.

Cate looked up puzzled and finally, realizing what Cheryl had said, started to laugh and then louder and from her stomach. And Cheryl laughed hard and harder. They all laughed. And finally fighting for control and air, they quieted down.

"Pretty sharp, aren't you Cheryl? Well, I'm not very experienced and I don't think he is either. We had had some punch at the prom and of course it was spiked. We were both rather comfortable. And he fell asleep. So what?"

"So what nothing. I didn't mean anything. I just pictured it and it was funny. I'm sorry, I should keep my mouth shut."

"That's okay, I understand. It does seem funny now. Anyway, I had to, you know, go to the bathroom. I didn't want to wake him up, so I slipped out of the car. I went behind a bush and pulled down my panty hose. I was squatting, holding my dress up, when he punched me in the back. I lost my breath. He pushed me hard onto the grass. He said he had a knife."

"Oh my God!" Cheryl was on her feet. She began pacing, her hands twisted around and around each other. She was watching Cate as she continued her story.

Mrs. A reached for Cate's hands. She felt the girl's cold fingers and covered them with her own. She looked into Cate's eyes whenever she looked up. She willed her to peace and control, so she could keep going.

"My skirt was already up. My pantyhose were down. He must have cut them, because he spread my legs. I couldn't do anything. I couldn't breath, you see, because he had punched me and my face was buried in the grass. I tried, but I couldn't.... I felt it go in and it was jamming me inside....Again...and again and...forever. I'm sorry," she cried from behind her hands.

"Sorry!" Cheryl was yelling. "Sorry! There's nothing for you to be sorry...! He's a pervert! A criminal! An animal! He...!" She suddenly sat down. She looked at Mrs. A helplessly. "Tell her Mrs. A. She doesn't have to feel sorry. She doesn't have to excuse her behavior. She had nothing to do with it. We all have to pee. That doesn't mean we have to get raped! Oh my God! I'd kill him!"

"Cheryl, I agree with you. But we have to help Cate now. We have to listen to her. We have to let her talk."

"He was grunting and swearing. He was so heavy and I couldn't breath. He had his hands on my shoulders and he held me still as he jammed. It was so hard to feel the force of his…. And then it was over. He punched me in the back again. He stood up and kicked me in the side. I lay there, waiting. I don't know for what or how long. But he had gone."

"Did you ever see him?" Mrs. A asked.

"No. When I caught my breath, I got up on my hands and knees and looked around. I could see the car and Jay sleeping in it. But I was alone. I stood up and something was trickling down my legs. It was blood. I panicked. I grabbed my pantyhose and stuffed them in there. I saw stains on my dress, but they were only grass. Right away, I thought, I can say I fell. I went back to the car and pushed Jay over. He fell on the floor of the passenger seat. I drove around until he was awake enough to tell him that I fell when I got out of the car to go to the bathroom and that I was driving home."

"You didn't tell him?" Mrs. A asked.

"No, I couldn't. He would feel so bad. And he didn't need to know. I knew I wouldn't tell anyone. I haven't told anyone. I couldn't."

"But you needed to. And I'm glad you finally did." Mrs. A soothed.

"Jesus," Cheryl said. "You didn't tell your mom?"

"She was waiting for me. She wanted to hear all about it, the prom I mean. I couldn't. She was so excited. I tried, I couldn't put her off. I was crying. Then she got worried. So I told her that I fell when I was going to the bathroom in the bushes and ruined my dress."

"And that was all you told her?" Cheryl was amazed.

"Well, she started to laugh. 'Is that all?' she said. 'That's nothing.' She said I was tired. She was right about that. She said I'd feel better in the morning. Boy, was she wrong about that. We've been fighting ever since. She won't leave me alone. And that's all I want."

"That explains a lot," Mrs. A said. "She's really been upset. Not with you, honey. But with the way things have been going between you. She wants to help. But don't you want to tell her?"

"NO! She's always going on about your 'girls.' How they were always in the way in the house. How much time you gave to 'them.' How stupid 'they' were. She calls them awful names. That's what she thinks of me now too. I should have taken care of it before this. But, I couldn't do anything. I couldn't think about anything. I feel like I am frozen in dirty ice."

"But the next morning…?" Cheryl asked.

"I told her I was wiped out…. I needed sleep. I had post prom cleanup. I spent all night in a corner of my room. I just stared at nothing. For hours. When the sun came up, I knew what I would do. I had a plan, a lie. A way to go on."

"I'm so sorry, Cate. I wish I had known," Mrs. A murmured.

"Well, having a plan and doing it are different. I wasn't strong. I wasn't thinking. I wasn't feeling. But when Mom figured it out, I knew I had to come here. I knew I had to do something."

"And I had a houseful."

"Yeh, that was a real bummer. But then I thought, I could maybe hide in the crowd. And besides, Ginny is great. She's a real supporter. I didn't know Cheryl was here, but she sure helped that first night."

"Sure, that's me. The scapegoat, the sacrificial lamb, the crucified sinner. Where's my 'Scarlet Letter?'"

"Really, Cheryl, it wasn't that bad, was it Grandma?"

"It was pretty bad. But Cheryl handled it well and like you said, that group is pretty supportive."

"Even for me. And they didn't even know me," Cheryl added.

"Is there anything else you want to tell?" Mrs. A asked Cate.

"I'm sorry this all happened. I've made a mess of my life. Everyone expected so much of me. And here I am."

"You can't control everything. Things happen. It's how you get through things that matter."

"And how do we get through these things?" Cheryl wondered.

"Well, you have to look at yourself. Your beliefs. Your hopes. There is an answer. If it's good for you, that's all that matters. You have to think about two things now. You and the baby. That's what you can do. When you decide, you have to arrange the rest. But at least you'll know what you have to arrange. But Cate, you said 'Here I am.' And 'here' you will always be. But you'll be stronger, more confident. You'll be wiser. More understanding. These troubles are part of life. We have them all the time, in all kinds of forms. We deal with them, the best we know how, and move on. We just hope we understand why we did what we did. So we don't go over and over it, so we can't 'move on.' I don't mean to be preaching. But I don't want you to be without hope."

"Life will go on, right? I don't mean to be ungrateful, but that sounds so trite, Mrs. A. 'Move on.' Do what you need to do. Don't let others convince you. It ain't that easy. This is big time. I'm just a kid."

"She's right, Grandma. She's right."

"Yes, she's right. But it still has to be done and soon. You're both at decision time in your pregnancy. I know you have done a lot of thinking and tomorrow, at the clinic, you'll get impartial information. And maybe some answers. And we'll talk again."

"Okay," Cheryl grumbled. She gathered her papers together and started upstairs. "You coming now?" she asked Cate.

"No. I want to talk with Grandma some more. Okay, Grandma?"

..*.*.*.*.*

"Let's get something to eat," Mrs. A headed into the kitchen.

"Can I have the last banana?" Cate followed through the door.

"Do you want peanut butter on that?"

"Mmmm, ya. And some of those pickles you make, you know, the watermelon ones."

"Spoken like a pregnant woman," Mrs. A laughed. She got the pickles out of the fridge and the peanut butter from the cupboard.

Cate scowled as she peeled the banana, grabbed a plate, a knife and fork. "There's that stereotype again. What are you going to have, Grandma?"

"Apple and cheese, I think. Will you have some?"

"That sounds good too."

The two sat at the table fixing their snacks and enjoying the company and the food.

"I didn't mean to hurt Mom, you know."

"And she knows that too. She's past the news and on to how to help. You have to let her in at least a little. She is your mother. And she's on your side."

"I don't know where she's coming from. She has this history with you. She says your 'girls' drove everyone away. Grandpa and Uncle Andrew and Aunt Katherine."

"My 'girls' did no such thing. I didn't neglect my family to help my 'girls.'"

"Why did Grandpa leave?"

Mrs. A was quiet. "It's hard to explain. He wouldn't ask. He never had a question. I'd say 'I have to…' and he would go along with whatever. He always did what I asked or needed him to do. He never asked for an explanation. He never got into it with me. He could always tell when I wanted or needed to talk and then he would move away, change the subject, or hug me, but he would never talk with me about it. I couldn't share with him. It was kind of lonely. For both of us."

"Why?"

"Afraid? Maybe he disapproved? Maybe he thought it was 'woman stuff?' He might have been disgusted or angry. I don't know. It didn't matter. He was the only one I could have talked to about it. But he didn't want to hear. So, it was my thing, not ours. Mine. It was between us all those years. And one day he left."

"Mom and Dad didn't talk much."

"Not that you heard. But maybe they did talk. Maybe it was something they learned. From us. By bad example. It's so much more. Two people have to work to stay together. And they have to work to let each other be separate. Sometimes I suppose one doesn't like the things the other one does. But how do you know? If nobody talks."

"There must have been signs."

"I suppose. But it was hiding all those years. Never coming up. Never spoken. We're still friends. You know that. We don't argue. He says he never argues. We don't ruin family get-togethers."

"I know. You guys are great. I guess no one knows why you broke up."

"Including me," Mrs. A laughed. "But you do the best you can. You can make it bad for everyone or you can handle it in a way that is at least good for most people."

"Mom seems to have taken it bad. She acts like she never had a home."

"Oh dear, that's a terrible way to feel. I have always loved her. And Al loves her. He just didn't want to live with me anymore. She was grown up.

The other kids were gone. He probably thought she could handle it."

"There's that cliché again," Cate said. She had finished her snack and placed her dishes in the sink.

"I'll get those," Mrs. A said. "You know, a cliché is a cliché because it is true and everyone knows it. We all have to 'handle' or 'deal' with things. We all have to 'move on.' Some just wait until there is no choice. Then they don't feel any blame. But looking at the problem, especially if it involves more than just you, and thinking of the possibilities can help you in the future. Problems like yours are here for your lifetime. You'll recall your decision over and over. Try to do what you can live with."

"I hear you Grandma, but how can I decide?"

"You just will, because you have to."

"But, Grandma, if I didn't do anything wrong, why do I have to pay for it?"

"Pay for it?"

"Well, it's like I'm the criminal. Even my mom. I know she doesn't know the whole story. I can imagine what she is thinking. About how I ended up pregnant. I hear her crying all the time. She's so ashamed of me."

"You can imagine all you want, but you will never know what she is thinking unless you talk with her and let her know what is going on. Believe me, she will understand more than you can ever know."

"Tell me, Grandma."

"It's not mine to tell."

"You're sounding awful mysterious."

"I don't mean to, honey. But I have to keep secrets. It's hard on me and my friends and family. But it can be a matter of life and death."

"Do you think it would help me to talk to her about it, you know, not feel so guilty, so dirty?"

"I believe talking about things helps. Dealing with it all alone, keeping it to yourself will not. Has it helped you so far, I mean not telling?"

The answer was almost inaudible. "No."

"Do you feel better now that Cheryl and I know?"

This time the answer was a soft sigh. "Yes."

"You have a lot of work to do to get over this. If you ever do? And we probably should talk with the police about it."

"Oh no! I won't. Everyone will find out. What can I tell them anyway? No!"

"But if what you can tell them helps with other cases, they might help get him. Putting everything together will make the picture clearer."

"What do you mean?"

"If I hide a piece of the puzzle, how can you finish it? It could be a sky piece, or an edge piece, or a very centerpiece. But they all make the picture don't they?"

"I suppose. Maybe I should talk to Mom before tomorrow. Do you think she would come over if we called?"

"You know where the phone is. It's up to you."

"But it's so late. She's probably sleeping. She's been so tired."

"Worry and crying tire you out, that's for sure. Maybe you can give her a little relief too. It has to be killing her, the way you have been suffering."

"I'm so angry!"

"But not at her."

"No. Yes! Yes! I am. I am angry at her. And me! I'm angry at me!"

"You had no choice. It happened. To you."

"Yeh, to me! And I have to pay! My life is ruined! My future is gone!"

"What affects you, affects everyone around you. Let them help you. Let them stand by you. Let them into your pain. We will share it and it will be more bearable. It will still be yours, but we can work together. We can pay it together. I really think you are starting to deal with it. I think it's time to bring your mom into it."

"Okay." The young woman stood. She straightened her sweatshirt and gathered her hair up, letting it drop back. She stood taller and taller. Quickly, she kissed her grandma on the cheek. "I'll be right back. Even if she doesn't come, I feel a lot better already."

She disappeared through the door to the kitchen. Mrs. A heard the phone dialing. The quiet voice was interrupted by crying but did not rise in anger. She heard her hang the phone up. There was a lot of nose blowing and the cupboard door closed after the tissues were thrown away. Mrs. A's eyes moistened as she pictured this baby girl. "It's not fair. She shouldn't have to pay. And she won't be alone. I swear it!"

"Well?" Mrs. A asked when Cate came back into the room.

"She's coming right over. With her pajamas even. She just had to let Jimmy know. She was crying."

"She wasn't the only one, was she?" Mrs. A blew her nose and returned the tissue to her pocket. "That must be how the Great Lakes were formed. From women's tears."

"How 'bout the ocean?"

"Really. Why don't we get our jammies on and I'll get the bedroom ready for your Mom, in case we do get any sleep."

"Should we get Cheryl up?"

"What do you think?" Mrs. A was impressed by the change in her "baby girl." She was on to the future now. There was hope in her. She was no longer the victim, but was in action mode.

"No. Let's keep it family. I like her a lot and we could be friends, but I need just family now. Okay?"

"Of course. This is your story."

Cha[ter 11

Mia let herself in. She had always kept her key. But with what went on in her childhood home, she rarely used it. Still, there could be emergencies, and her mother might need her. So, she kept it in the bottom of her purse.

Cate was just coming down the stairs. In her pajamas. Those with the white clouds on the bright blue sky. But more than that, there was the bright face of her child. The face she hadn't seen for ages. "Sweetheart!"

Cate finished the steps in three leaps. "Mom!" She whispered loudly as she realized that Cheryl was still sleeping. She had managed to get into the room they shared and grab her pajamas without waking her roommate. She had changed in the bathroom and washed her face and brushed her teeth. How long had it been since she really felt these activities? She noticed how dirty her hair was. When had she last washed it? She didn't know how long she had been staring at herself when she heard the front door opening. She kicked her clothes into the corner. She could pick them up later. She started down the stairs and spotted her mom looking up at her. She looked so tired. She looked so old. "Mom," she whispered loudly.

They left Mia's bag by the door and went arm and arm into the kitchen. "I don't think I want any coffee, honey, but is there anything else to drink?"

..*.*.*.*.*

Mrs. A came down the stairs just as they returned with sodas. "Do you want anything, Grandma?"

"Sure. I'll take one of those too."

As Cate left to get the Diet Rite, Mrs. A gave her daughter a big hug. "Oh, Mom," Mia breathed.

"It's going to work out. You've been so patient. But it's going to be all right."

"How the hell can it be all right! You can't fix everything you know."

"Maybe we can, together, honey."

"I put yours in a glass, Grandma. Okay?" The brighter Cate reappeared from the kitchen. She watched as the two older women separated. She wished they could have stayed together a little longer so she could have joined them.

"I'm going to sit here, so I can put my feet up," Mrs. A said.

Cate plopped down onto the floor and grabbed a pillow from the couch. Her mother curled up in the farther corner of the couch. "Want another pillow?"

"Yeh, thanks." Silence shrouded the room. Cate found something very interesting about her feet. Mrs. A sat with her eyes closed. Mia stared at her daughter. Then she glanced over at her mother. "Mom! Are you sleeping or praying?"

"I think 'praying' describes it best," she answered. "I was wondering how to start this conversation, but I decided it wasn't up to me."

"You're right, Grandma. It's up to me. Mom, it's my 'story.' I need to tell you."

"And I need to hear it," her mother answered.

Mrs. A sat with her eyes closed as Cate pretty much repeated the facts of the story she had told her grandma and Cheryl earlier. Every once in a while, she would open her eyes and look at one or the other, especially when she heard her daughter's voice.

"Prom night? I didn't…." Mia started to get up to go to her daughter. Cate raised her hand to stop her.

"That's not important, Mom. None of what happened is important. I don't know how any of it could have been prevented. I mean, we just wanted to talk about the dance and the kids and the music and the clothes, you know, wind down. We had a fun time, really. It was stupid to park there, but the other kids talked about making out there, so even though we didn't plan on making out, we went there. What's wrong with that?"

"Nothing, Punkin. You didn't do anything wrong, except…."

Mrs. A's eyes were open now.

"Except what?" challenged Cate. Her suddenly rigid spine made her taller. Her arms crushed the pillows to her chest. Her chin stuck out, waiting to fight off the blow she expected from her mother.

"Except, you didn't tell me then, so I could help you right away."

"I suppose you thought it was all about you." Cate shot back.

"No, but I knew it was about us. I knew you were angry. Angry at me. I didn't know why. So, I assumed it was mother teenage daughter conflict, like in the books. But it never let up. It got worse, whether I gave you space or pressed you. And I felt you were self-destructing. Right before my eyes. I felt hopeless. Helpless. So, yes it was about me. I was worried sick. For you."

"Well, you didn't do anything about it, did you?" Cate was looking for a reason to be mad at her mother. If it wasn't her fault, if she couldn't be angry with herself, maybe she could blame her mother.

"Didn't I? I tried to get you interested again. Shopping? A movie? A book? The lake? Whatever I tried, no go. Just anger and withdrawal. I didn't know why, but I knew you hated me."

"Why would I hate you, Mom?"

Mrs. A sat up. She put her feet on the floor and leaned into the little group. "Maybe it's time you told your story, Mia?"

..*.*.*.*.*

Cate was looking at her grandma, and slowly turned to look at her mother. "You have a story, Mom?"

"What was it Ginny said? We all have a story. Mine's a little different. But I have learned that it wasn't my fault. I have learned that good can come from anything and everything. I have learned to forgive myself. Well, most of the time. Because it ended up all right. Grandma promised me it would be all right. Didn't you?"

"However it ends up, it's always 'all right.'"

"Not when you're planning suicide," Cate said.

Now Mia was sitting up. Her hands were clasped together. Her eyes were on her daughter. "Were you thinking that?"

"Well, it was one way out."

"Your grandma told me that was selfish. Like my mom."

"Like Grandma Karen?"

"Umhmm. She felt hopeless."

"We think.... We assume she felt hopeless or she wouldn't have done it. I was there to help. In the end, I did help. But I lost my sister," Mrs. A spoke with despair.

"Remember, Mom, when I had you take me there?" Mia asked.

"That was too gruesome." Mrs. A paused. "I hated doing that. But I think it was good that we went. I had never wanted to know. But it made me understand her hopeless feelings even better."

"Yeh. What a terrible place. Such an awful end. It's hard to understand how she could do it," Mia slowly shook her head.

"She was always so happy. Sometimes I hated her for being so happy," Mrs. A said. "She got everything she wanted. Clothes, music lessons, contact lenses. She went to two proms. And the homecoming dance. And then, Bill. So good looking. Charming. We all fell for him. How could she do it? I still don't get it. What a terrible place...."

"I thought about doing that," Cate whispered.

"That's why I had Grandma take me there. I thought I would do it there too. Wasn't that romantic?" Mia said, her voice full of sarcasm. "Mother and daughter end it at the same place, a generation apart."

"I was going to go there too," Cate added. Both mother and grandmother whimpered behind the fingers covering their mouths.

"It was a horrible place," continued Mrs. A. "First we went to the intersection below and put a piece of paper where we thought they found her. It was a gray day, but we don't know what the weather was for her. And it's been thirty years since...."

They all respected the pause that settled over them. They were all settling down again, slowly, painfully. They took the same seats, except Cate took the other corner of the couch from her mother. They both had their feet up and were almost touching toes.

"Think it looked the same, only older. Even more decrepit. I'd been through there many times, even before.... Well, there's nothing new there. People try to keep things up, but it's an old river community. Lots of immigrants passed through there. A lot of history. It's pretty run down now. Shabby...," Mrs. A stopped.

"And a lot of people used it like my mother did. Not the neighborhood, but the bridge. If you know about those things, you can't help but feel hopeless and depressed standing there," Mia explained. "I had never been there before, I didn't know about the others. I learned that some of them, they found way down river. Some on far banks in Iowa," Mia was talking very softly.

"Those were the ones who chose the water. But my sister wanted to be sure, I guess. She chose the land. She chose the middle of the intersection. She didn't want to miss. She didn't want to wreck anybody else's life. She wanted to be found. Oh, I don't really know what she wanted, she didn't leave a note. Just flew off the railing."

"Did someone see her…do it?" Cate asked.

"No one came forward. You know, it was in the paper of course, even a picture. I didn't keep it. I couldn't look at it and I didn't want you to look at it."

"I did find it. I went to the Historical Society and found it on file. I have a copy. I do look at it. Often."

"Why?" choked Mrs. A.

"I have to. I try to understand. She was my mom."

"Can I see it?" Cate asked. Her grandmother stared at her in surprise.

Her mother said, "Sure, if you need to."

"Mia!" Mrs. A exclaimed.

"Why not? She has a right to her history, Mom, just like I do mine. You can do what you think is right for me or her, but it really is our decision in the end. Isn't that what you've always said? Isn't that what you say to your 'girls?'"

"I think I'd like to see the picture. Some day, I may go there too, but right now, I don't have time." Cate paused. "I have to make a decision. I don't think it will be the same as hers. Although, it was an option before, you know. Were you pregnant, Mom?"

"Yes, but your grandma didn't know at the time."

"I knew something was horribly wrong," Mrs. A said. "I knew that my beautiful daughter was suffering. She didn't bathe. I couldn't get her to wash her hair. One morning she came down with most of it cut off. She wouldn't go to get it shaped. She wouldn't let me touch it. Well, she wasn't letting me touch her at all. She sat around the house. She curled up in a ball and stared at nothing. She didn't eat. If I got her to eat, I could hear her throwing it up in the bathroom right after. She skipped school on nice days and on bad days, she told me she was too sick to go. She wore baggy clothes and even though she wasn't eating, they were beginning to tighten in the middle. I thought something was terribly wrong. I couldn't get anywhere with her. It was more than teen hostility. It was hatred. Of me, but more so of herself."

"Sounds familiar," Cate murmured.

"I tried to figure out what had changed. When it had changed. And, of course, why. I realized that she no longer asked about her dad. She never went with him anymore. He didn't ask for her, but was taking the boys hunting or fishing or whatever, a lot. This had been going on for quite a while. Before, he never had time for the boys and they went with Grandpa or Grandpa and Andrew. And you," she turned to Mia, "had spent almost every weekend with your dad. I thought maybe you missed him or that you were jealous. I thought maybe he hurt your feelings. But this was much stronger, more scary to me. I thought you would talk to me about it eventually. I remembered how you used to dress up for your time with your dad. You talked about the things you did together. The movies and dinners. The shopping and long drives and stops at the little resorts. You were always so excited. Happy to see him and go with him. He never came into the house. You would literally race out to the car, throw your bag in the back, jump in and the two of you would tear off. Not even a wave. You almost always came back with a gift, or new clothes. I was so happy for you. It had taken quite a while for you two to establish yourselves, to establish a relationship."

"So, why did it end, Mom?"

"I got my period."

"What?" Cate looked from one to the other. Mrs. A was rubbing her forehead. Her nose was running. Her eyes were squeezing back teardrops that refused to be squeezed.

Mia continued. "Oh, I didn't tell him right away. I was embarrassed. I was afraid I wouldn't be his little girl anymore. But one weekend, I had it and I was wearing a pad. And when he saw it he went crazy. He took me home. I didn't know why. That next weekend he didn't come for me, or the next. It was a month later. I guess he thought he could count and that it would be safe. I was so happy to be with him again, I didn't even think about it. But we went to monthly visits. I loved him so much, I could hardly stand it. But he said that it had to be that way. He said he hated condoms. I didn't even know what those were."

"Oh my God, Mom."

"It's too much for you. I told Grandma. But she thought we needed to do this. I didn't want you to know. It was too horrible. But maybe she was right. You have your horrible. I have mine. You are completely innocent…."

"So are you," Mrs. A rose and reached for her daughter. Mia stopped her with the stay away arm gesture.

"Don't, Mom! I loved him. I loved doing it with him. I believed he loved me and this was how he shared with me. I didn't know anything. I didn't want to know anything. We were having such a great time. In between, he'd take me to the park and push me on the swing or we'd ride the merry-go-round. We both loved the zoo. And in the museum, he would show me pictures that kind of made me blush, but he would always say that it was okay to be shy. He said we weren't the only people to be so lucky and happy with each other. I felt so special. And then I started to feel dirty. He didn't want to hold me. He didn't kiss my forehead anymore. He didn't enter me anymore. He showed me alternatives that would satisfy us. It wasn't the same. It was mechanical. It wasn't love and cuddling and laughter. We didn't go anywhere. He started to just leave me at his place and come back late. He was usually drunk. Sometimes so drunk, he wouldn't be careful. I was actually happier on those days."

"How long?"

"Oh God. What? Five? Maybe six years, Mom?

"You never could tell me when it started. And I couldn't tell. But it was after your mother died. I know she never would have left you if she had known he was like that."

"I can't believe it. It's too horrible. How could he? His own daughter?"

"I was there. I was his. I thrived because of it. He made me feel so special, so loved. I didn't know it was wrong. But I did it. Willingly."

"No! Mia! We've talked about this. You've talked with your therapist. I know you have. You were a child. Maybe he didn't force you, so you thought you were willing. But he primed you. He brought you along. He made you compliant. All children, not only those who have lost a mother, all children want to be special, to be happy, to make their parents happy. He was the evil one. He knew it was wrong. He knew how to keep you from telling. You don't even remember how he manipulated you. He did it all lovingly. I don't know how he got you to not tell anyone. I don't know how I missed it all those years."

"Yes, all those years. Happy years. And then, hard years of wondering why things had changed. Why did I feel so unspecial. So dirty. So unloved where I once was a princess so much loved. I heard the girls at school talking. I was so mixed up. I asked my teacher. But she got all nervous and said that was something I should ask my mother. How could I do that? Nobody could help me. I knew you loved me and I hated you for it. How could you love me? Me!"

"So, then your mom started asking about her mother. I answered her questions, but she wouldn't let me in. A couple questions, a couple answers. Boom! She was gone. To her room. Outside. Down the basement. Gone! If I asked her a question, the silent treatment. The glare. Then gone!"

"I finally got her to take me there. Where Mom jumped. We went up on the bridge. It is so high. Really. Such a long way down. We almost couldn't find our piece of paper. It took a while. I don't think you were even trying, Mom."

"I couldn't focus. I was trying not to cry. I kept wanting to let it go, to scream. I was in such pain. But it was about you that day."

"We finally were able to see. To picture what she did. I tried to imagine doing it. The railing was chest high to me. She would have had to climb up. There was a lamp post just there above the paper. That had to make it easier to get up and over. And something to hang on to in case you changed your mind and wanted to climb back down. If you wanted to."

"I remember, you said, 'Maybe she slipped, Mom?' I said 'Yes, maybe.' I couldn't believe she could do it. I didn't want to believe she could do it. God! What an awful day! Even worse than the day I heard about it. I had already lost her and I knew I was losing you. I kept my hand on you the whole time. Remember we hung on to each other for a long time. I was so afraid. I was desperate. I had promised to take care of you and here you were. I thought I knew your plans. I was trying to figure out how to stop you. And then you said, 'I wouldn't do it.' Firm and strong. You convinced me. You looked at me and said it again, 'Never, I wouldn't do that.'"

"No, not even being pregnant. One thing he did for me was to make me feel special. And even though things had changed and I felt dirty, I still felt special somehow. I felt some hope. I thought I could make him love me again especially with the baby. I didn't know what he did to my mother. He said he loved me like her. I was confused about what was happening, but I thought it would be all right. I thought, 'I'm not going to do that. I'll tell him about the baby and we'll be all right. It would be all right.'"

"I hated him," said Mrs. A.

"I loved him," answered Mia.

"Mom. He was so evil. He was more evil than that guy…. I mean…. Years! His own daughter. How could your mom have stayed with him? He is…what do they call it…? Anything he does or wants is okay."

"Amoral. Evil." Mrs. A growled.

"What about Randy and Bob? What did he do to them? No wonder you never wanted him to come around. I never got that. Your own dad!" Cate said.

"Even before your mom started to tell me…. And believe me it took many years for her to tell it all. But right away, as my suspicions grew, I put obstacles in his way. I dragged her with me everywhere. I made sure he didn't come around. I didn't know what he had done…. I mean, who could imagine…."

"I didn't have any friends. He said I didn't need silly children for friends. I was too mature. I had him. He was my best friend. I believed he was."

"This is so awful. I…. I can't…. How…? Grandma, we're out of tissues. I'm going to run upstairs, go potty and get some." She stopped next to her mom and gave her a crushing hug before dashing up the stairs.

Mia's eyes were wide open. She turned to her mother. "You knew. You knew how she would take it."

"I hoped I knew how she would take it. But I didn't really. She's a good girl. She's smart. This has her all confused. She's in an awful situation. But she's okay too. She's been loved too. Except, you've loved her in a way that is good for her.

You've been able to love her after all your hard work. It's worked out all right. You know?"

They were both wiping their eyes when Cate came back down the stairs. She passed the tissue box around and settled back onto the couch. This time her toes actually smushed up against her mother's toes. Strength flew both ways along that connection.

"Mom, we have a lot of talking and listening to do, you and I…," Cate started.

Mia nodded and smiled. "But right now, I need to ask you the question. The baby?"

Mrs. A sucked in her breath. Cate was right, this was the question. So much more had to be said. But her granddaughter knew what was important.

"The baby…," Mia started and then looked over at her mother. "The baby is your cousin Lisa."

"You mean, Lisa is my sister?"

"Yes. Your sister."

"Wait a minute! Is she my aunt? Mom's sister?"

"Let's not go too far with this," Mrs. A broke in.

"You're right. That's cruel. I'm sorry, Mom. But it's so cool, a sister. I can't believe it. How did you…? How did you decide?"

"It was easy. I waited too long. It was too late. I was glad. I never knew what all Grandma's girls were doing, but I had no choice."

"But how did you handle it? What did you arrange, Grandma?

"Well, I told you I had to get her away from that bastard…I'm sorry honey."

"That's okay, Mom, I know your opinion pretty well."

"Well, that's mine too," Cate added.

"There's got to be a lot more talk here. But I took her on a tour with me and Mary, Lisa's mom. Mary told everyone she was pregnant. We didn't really know when your mom was due. So we kind of guessed how pregnant Mary should be. It was a car trip. People thought it was great. Get your mom away and get her out of her funk. Show her the sights. 'You'll all enjoy it,' people said. And Mary had been having a tough time at college and needed a break. And she and Pete had agreed to take the baby as their own. Except for why we were going, we tried to enjoy it."

"Yeh, enjoy," Mia said. "We went from one sight to another. It's a good thing we took pictures, because I was sure unconscious the whole trip."

"No, you weren't, honey."

"I sure was. We'd talk. I'd cry. We'd stop to eat. I'd cry. We drove all over the southwest and I cried the whole way."

"But remember, we would stop for a couple days and hike around. The desert is beautiful and there aren't a lot of people around."

"Not much of anything around."

"See, you do remember something," Mrs. A laughed. "We were in Santa Fe when her time came. The social worker at the hospital helped us. She put Mary and Pete's name on the birth certificate. We called home with the good news about Mary and the baby. Said we were surprised that the baby came so soon. We would rest for a week before starting back. We got our act together and the four of us came back. Then the really tough times began."

"She doesn't have to hear about that now, maybe never."

"You're right, Mia. We've had enough for one night," Mrs. A stated. "You certainly did that well, both of you."

"I have so much to learn. Thank you, Grandma. And especially you, Mom. I can't believe that happened to you. And you never told anyone."

"Oh yes I did." She looked at her mother. "And she knew how to do what I needed even though I was totally lost. It was the best thing. I've been able to watch Lisa grow and change and become a fantastic person and mom."

"Does she know?" Cate asked.

"I don't know. I don't think so. We've never talked about it. She's pretty quiet around me," Mia answered.

Mrs. A looked puzzled. "You know, Mia, Mary and Pete asked us not to tell. And you have to keep mum too, sweetheart. It's been easier for your mom this way, right Mia?"

"It's never been easy. Nothing has been easy. It was too much to ever get over. I just keep moving. And now I'm moving up to bed. Come on 'little Mommy.'"

"Don't call me that!" Cate shot back. And mounted the stairs.

Grandmother and mother were left to look at each other. Mrs. A turned back into the living room to turn off the lights and Mia followed her daughter up the stairs.

..*.*.*.*

It didn't matter what you knew or lived through, there was always something to knock you over, shake your world. But lately Mrs. A was feeling beaten. Al was still helping her with the bills, but the house needed so much. And now the fire. No! She wouldn't think about that yet. She had to deal with today. Cheryl and Cate. One a stranger, the other her own blood. And she could never rest about Mia. The years of therapy. The self-destructive behaviors. The long side trips of her life. She had married David. Cate and Jimmy came along and she seemed to find her way. She had finally found something to structure her life around. She had found work at the bank that satisfied her. Paid good benefits too. And as that all settled down in her life, Mrs. A believed she would be all right. Then David had left. Mia had nothing to say. She stated that she would be fine. They would be fine. She stayed in the house with the kids. She kept them on a tight leash, but she loved them and let their grandma spoil them. Mrs. A didn't know too much about her daughter's life, and Cate was closer than Jimmy. But then, he was fifteen and into friends and sports. She went to as many activities for both the kids as she could. They were always welcome in her house. And they took advantage often to come and visit. And bring their friends.

Andrew's kids weren't as close, but then Chicago wasn't close. She saw them as often as she could. Two, three weeks at a time, when she could afford the flight. He'd fly her down one or two times a year. But more often when the kids were young. Once they started school, she didn't see them as much.

Kathryn and her family were out East. Their place was very nice, but small. She used to see more of them too, but now the kids resented her coming. One of them would have to give up a room for her. And besides, they were in school now and had activities after school and their own friends. She missed them. And calling was so expensive. She and her daughter talked once a month or so. Kathryn seldom responded to her occasional letters. She was so busy with the kids and her career.

Sometimes she thought about moving. But Kathryn's place was too small. And Mia would still be here. And how could she move. The girls knew how to find her here. And they still came to her. So, she would stay here.

She turned off the lights and headed up the stairs herself.

Chapter 12

Of course, Cheryl was the first one up. She had gone to bed earlier. She tiptoed down the stairs. She had looked at the clock when Cate finally crawled into bed. So, she knew she hadn't had much sleep yet. She went to the front door to get the paper and looked for a moment at the quiet street and remembered how it had looked with the fire engines and the police cars clogging the road. She pictured the clusters of neighbors and kids who watched as Mrs. A was carried out on a stretcher to the ambulance. They quickly left, almost disappointed that the sirens hadn't been turned on when the ambulance pulled away. That seemed like ages ago. And now, today, more excitement. She knew that people picketed the clinic. Even her own parents. They tried to stop people from going in. They could get nasty sometimes. She hoped there wouldn't be anyone she knew. She didn't want anything to stop her from what she had to do.

As she turned back inside, she saw Cate's mom coming down the stairs. Their eyes met for just a moment. Cheryl was confused by her feelings as the older woman stepped off the stairs. She quickly remembered her manners and said "Good morning, Mrs. Mayer. Did you sleep well?"

"Not long enough," she stated. "We were up half the night. How about you?"

"Great, really. I brought the paper in."

"I think I'll get the coffee started right away. The others will be up soon. What time will you all be leaving?" They were walking into the kitchen together.

Mrs. A came down the stairs as they headed for the kitchen. "Oh, no!"

"What is it, Mrs. A?" Cheryl asked.

"What's the matter, Mom?"

They looked out the door and saw the flat tires on Mia's car. Three of them. They looked at each other. "Damn," said Mia. "I forgot about 'nails on the driveway.'"

"I never even thought about it last night. And they hadn't done it in a while. I'll call Fred at the garage. He'll take care of it." Mrs. A turned inside to make the phone call.

"What's going on, Mom," Cate came out to the stoop. "Holy crap!"

"Watch your mouth young woman," her mother snapped. But she put her arm around her daughter's shoulders.

Cate pulled away and jammed past her into the house. She huffed loudly as she passed the returning Mrs. A.

"Fred will be here soon. But don't feel so bad. I'll pay for it. At least they've stopped putting them in the street gutter. My neighbors really got mad the last time and called the police. They stopped doing it after that. For a long while, nothing happened, but now…." Mrs. A breathed a deep sigh.

"You certainly won't. I can pay for it myself. You're in enough trouble already. You aren't going to use your few dollars to help me when I knew better. I guess I was just too upset last night and didn't think about it. I just pulled into the driveway without thinking. So I'll pay, thank you." Mia walked out to her car and stooped to pick up things from the driveway. "Nails all right. Lots of them. All over the drive." She started picking them up.

As she was cleaning the driveway, Fred's tow truck pulled up. She waved with both hands to prevent him from coming into the driveway yet. Mrs. A walked out to join them and to help pick up the nails. Then they watched as Fred jacked up the car and removed the three tires.

"Should I put on the spare? Or just wait until I get them all fixed?"

"Might as well wait. I can't go anywhere anyway," Mia answered.

"You know, it's funny. All those nails around, but these tires were all punctured in the same place. Near the top." Fred took his cap off, ran his hand over his hair and put it back on.

"Really," Mrs. A wondered. "What do you think that means, Fred?"

"Looks more like somebody hammered 'em in. Not like you ran over the nails. Well, no matter, I have to fix 'em at the shop. I'll be back after lunch."

"That doesn't make sense. Why would they hammer the nails and then throw nails around?"

"Mom, he probably doesn't know what he's talking about."

"I'm not so sure. He's helped us with this so many times over the years. I think he knows a hammered hole from a 'drive over a nail' hole."

"Well maybe they hammered my tires and threw the nails to get some other car. It just proves, Mom, that you're not safe here. You really need to give this all up. Really!" Mia tried to turn her mother so that she could see into her eyes. But Mrs. A continued to watch Fred with a very puzzled face. "You're probably right," she said as she waved good-bye to Fred.

"Well, we're all up. What time will we be leaving?" Mia and Cheryl were walking into the kitchen together. Mia reached for the coffee pot and began to fill it with water.

"The first appointment is at ten thirty. I don't know how far it is. But I'm ready. There's no bag needed today. I wouldn't know what to bring anyway." Cheryl said.

"Oh, you'll learn a lot today. Have you made your decision?"

"Mrs. A says we should be open and listen to everything today. She will talk with us again afterward. So, I guess, I think I know, but maybe I'll hear something new today." Cheryl shrugged her shoulders.

"It is a baby, you know." Mia was staring at her now. "I don't know or care how far along you are. It is a baby now. Right now!"

"I.... I mean. I hear you," the young woman stuttered.

"Good. You only get one chance to make a mistake or to save a life. It will hang over you the rest of your life, you know."

Mrs. A entered the room with her eyes glaring at her daughter. "Mia, I've asked you not to...."

"What? Don't I get an opinion? Someone has to talk for the babies."

"Mia," Mrs. A tried to calm her daughter. "Were you thinking of coming with?"

"Of course," Mia answered.

"Not!" Cate added strongly as she came into the kitchen.

"What?" her mother asked.

"You're not coming."

"But, you need me. I'm your mother."

"You're my mother. And I need you. But not today. Not for this. I know what you think. I've heard it my whole life. 'My mother this. Grandma's girls that.' Mom, you have to back off. I need to do this myself."

"But you're letting Grandma…."

"No. I'm not letting Grandma anything. I'm using Grandma, because she's someone who knows. She has information I need. I really don't know what I'll do. I don't need to know yet. I need to understand. I need to be objective. You're not objective. And after what we talked about last night, I really don't get it at all."

"What do you mean?"

"Well, you said yourself, you had no choice. Besides being illegal, you said it was too late to do anything. Things are so different now. People have changed. I can do so much more than you could. I have so much more to think about."

"But…"

"No, Mom! Please, no more." Cate yanked open the refrigerator and grabbed for the juice. Cheryl had been watching the mother daughter encounter and quickly turned away. She opened the cupboard and took down four juice glasses. Mia turned her back trying to stop the tears. She continued making the coffee, but only managed to spill water and grounds on the counter. Mrs. A moved over beside her, almost touching, but still giving her daughter the space she needed in her misery.

Cate and Cheryl sat down at the table. Each poured herself a glass of juice. They stared at the glasses in their hands. Mrs. A added cereal bowls, milk, cereal and spoons to the tabletop. The girls helped themselves and silently ate. Mrs. A joined them at the table. Mia stood at the counter waiting for the coffee to brew.

"Okay. I know Grandma will take care of you. I would really like to be there. I don't want you to have to go alone, you know."

"I know, Mom. I'm not going alone. But I don't want you to go with me."

"Well, I give up, I guess. But I love you so much."

"I know, Mom. Go home…. Love me enough to go home. Please." The "please" was a whisper. No one moved. No one even blinked.

Finally, Mia shuddered. "I think I'll have just a little coffee before I go. Anyone else? Wait! My car. I'll have to wait until Fred gets back." The room came alive again as Mrs. A held up her cup and Mia filled it. The girls shoved their chairs away from the table and got up to go. Cate turned to her mother and gave her a quick hug. "Thanks, Mom," she said. As they both left the room, Cate said to her grandma, "Call us when you're ready."

Mother and daughter sat at the table over their coffee. Mrs. A reached over to cover her daughter's hand. Mia pulled away.

"I don't want her to do this, Mom. Don't let her do it. It's my first grandchild."

"Really, Honey, I don't think she's decided anything yet."

"Don't be too sure. I thought our talk last night would have changed her resolve. But there's no change."

"Her resolve is to stay strong. She is wound pretty tight right now. She's walking a balance beam, like she did as a kid. Remember how she used to concentrate so she wouldn't fall off. That's what she's doing now, Sweetheart. She's concentrating. She is on that beam alone, you know. She can't even hear advice now. At least not from us."

"Not from me, you mean. Not from her own mother! God damn you, Mother. You and your 'girls.' You and your 'mission.' She would listen to me if it wasn't for you. I gotta get out of here." She almost ran from the room and up the stairs.

..*.*.*.*.*.

Mrs. A sat a long time alone with her coffee. This wasn't the first time someone had screamed those words at her. Not even the first time someone in her family had said those words. "Her mission." What was that supposed to mean? Really, is that what it had been? Certainly something she believed in. Enough to give her life to it. Enough to lose her husband for. Her children. It controlled everything. She couldn't move, because the girls wouldn't be able to find her. She couldn't have a listed number, or get mail at the house, because the "anti's" might find her. She was always aware of unusual people around her. Fear was a constant in her life. She never went on a vacation. Well, she couldn't really afford it anyway. Since Al left, she was very poor. He still helped her out every once in a while, but her social security barely kept her going. If the kids didn't keep up with the birthday and Christmas checks, she would be in deep trouble. Actually, she was in deep trouble. She was considering a boarder, but that would leave less room for the girls. Although, she rarely had more than one at a time. And it seemed to be working out with Cheryl and Cate bunking together.

But the morning was moving along and she and the girls better get moving too. She hoped the picketers weren't there already. They should have gotten earlier appointments. She put the coffee cups in the sink with the girls' dishes and went into the living room. She called to the girls and reached for her purse. She found the keys and turned to look at the two girls as they came bounding down the stairs. So healthy. So young. Her heart was breaking.

"We might as well head out. Have you got your questions and pencils?" The girls nodded. A look of fear showed in both their faces for just a moment. Mrs. A's smile and jaunty "Let's get going then!" chased the fear away and they were two young girls on an excursion. Maybe they'd have lunch out.

..*.*.*.*.*

When they drove up to the clinic, there was only one picketer visible. An older man in a plaid flannel shirt. He had on khaki pants and brown shoes. The sign he held had red letters next to a picture of an infant. "Don't kill me!" it spelled. They didn't look at each other. Cheryl stared at the man. And Cate looked at the building they would be entering. Mrs. A backed the car into a parking spot as close to the building as possible. She had no idea what would be going on when they came out.

She and the girls got out of the car. The man started to move closer to them. Mrs. A held up her arm. "Stop!" she shouted. Surprised, the man did stop. Mrs. A guided the girls ahead of her and into the building before he recovered. He must be new, Mrs. A thought. He certainly wasn't as aggressive as most of them were. The law requiring the twenty-four hour wait had really encouraged the picketers. They took pictures of people going in and the next few days they would be looking for the women who came back, knowing that they were coming for a procedure. It was like shining a spotlight on the women. "Hey look! This is the one! Get her!" But it was the law and she did her best to guide the girls and let them know what might happen. She couldn't save them from the "antis," so she tried to prepare them. But how could you prepare anyone for the behavior picketers exhibited.

They were standing at the reception desk. A young woman sat in a small window. She was on the phone, but looked up and smiled at the girls and raised her index finger in a "just a moment" gesture. She finished her phone conversation and directed her full attention to the two.

"How can I help you?" she asked. "Oh, hi, Mrs. A. I didn't see you there right-a-way." The girls gave their names, which were then checked off a list. They were handed clipboards and pencils to fill out their "histories." They followed the receptionist's wave toward the chairs along the wall. Mrs. A led the way and they were soon seated, on either side of Mrs. A, printing away, as required, on the forms.

Occasionally they showed each other their answers and discussed entries with Mrs. A. Cheryl's hair kept falling in her face, and needed constant attention. Mrs. A sat rather primly between the two, responding as needed. Her purse sat on her lap and her hands rested on her purse. She kept her eyes on the front door and the receptionist's window.

Cate sat further back in her chair. In between questions on the form, she chewed on the pencil she had been given. She had fewer questions and was done first. She walked up to the receptionist and handed the clipboard over.

"Just take a seat. We're on schedule. In fact, somebody canceled an appointment, so it won't be long."

Cate returned to her seat. "Somebody canceled an appointment." She sounded surprised and concerned. "Is that why they make you wait a day? They want you to cancel?"

"Sure," Cheryl responded. "Anything to stop you."

"You know," said Mrs. A. "They do a lot of things here. Counseling, birth control, education, disease prevention. A lot of things. Didn't the desk have brochures? You two should go look for material. It's free. It could help you now and in the future. Cheryl are you about done?"

"Yeh, I'm done, but I don't know…."

"Are you scared?" Cate asked in a snarling way, almost like a dare. "Think they're going to change your mind? Get a clue! They can't do anything you don't want. They're not going to tie you down. You can leave at any time. Right?" She looked at Mrs. A.

"She's absolutely right. Today is counseling only. Then if you want, you make another appointment."

"But," Cheryl started. "But, could we go in together?"

Mrs. A smiled and patted her hand. "No. If your mom or dad were here or your boyfriend. They could be involved if you wanted, but we can't be in there with you. There are privacy rules and laws. And you don't want to be influenced by other people's opinions. This is your lifetime decision. We can talk afterward if you want. In fact, I hope we talk afterward. Take your clipboard up now, Cheryl, and the both of you look over the materials there by the desk. Some reading material will help pass the time anyway." As the girls walked away, she opened her purse and took out a paperback for her own reading.

Cheryl handed her clipboard and pen to the receptionist who smiled warmly at both of them. "Take a look at the materials here. You can take whatever you want. It's all free. It's about a fifteen minute wait now." She smiled at the two of them. Friendly. Warm. Cheryl shivered and turned quickly to the material display.

She and Cheryl took a little time looking over the brochures, even giggling about some of them. They pointed at this one and that one, and selected another, finally coming back each with a few of them to read. They sat down, sagged into comfort and began reading.

Other women came in, checked in, filled out forms, perused the materials, and sat down to wait. Others came out through the door that led to the exam rooms. Some headed immediately out. Some stopped at the front desk. Some stopped, inspected the materials, took a few with as they left. Time passed quickly.

"Cate Mayer?" the woman with a clipboard asked. All three looked up. Cate stood up and followed the clipboard woman through the door. The other two watched her go and looked at each other. Mrs. A patted Cheryl's knee and they returned to their reading.

Ten minutes later, the same clipboard woman called Cheryl's name and Mrs. A was left alone. She closed her book and continued to watch the front door and the desk. The other women also stared into space or studied their shoes or hands. It was a hard place to concentrate.

..*.*.*.*.*.

Cate returned first. She stopped at the desk on her way. She came back with a small white card which she stuffed in her pocket. She plopped next to Mrs. A, folded her arms and glared at the door, daring anyone to speak with her. They sat in silence waiting for Cheryl to reappear. Twenty minutes passed before she came. She also stuffed something into her pocket as she came toward them. She stood in front of them, a small smile on her face.

"Are we ready?" Mrs. A asked looking from one to the other.

"Guess so," said Cheryl.

"Let's go," declared Cate.

As they headed for the door, Mrs. A said, "There are a few more picketers waiting for us. Just stay close behind me. Don't look at them, and don't say anything." Smiling, she opened the door and stepped out into the bright sunlight, the girls on either side, just a little behind, almost touching. Like two ducklings following their mother on their first excursion onto the water.

The picketers had been watching for them and they lifted their signs and Bibles. A man began speaking or maybe he was praying. Another man held up a sign with a bloody picturc of a fetus tangled in its umbilical cord and placenta. A young woman held up a sign of a healthy toddler which she had stored in the stroller holding her own healthy toddler. An older woman dropped to her knees and began singing the children's hymn "Jesus loves the little children, all the children of the world...." No one stepped toward them, but they had to cross the grass area to get to the parking lot. There another man and woman stood blocking their way. They tried to hand them materials. Cheryl refused, but Cate took what she was offered and added them to her collection from inside the clinic.

Mrs. A hurried to unlock the passenger door. The others from the sidewalk had joined the parking lot group too and they were all shouting at once.

"Don't do it!"

"There's help!"

"It's murder!"

"You're not alone!"

"Whore!"

"You don't want to be a killer!"

"Killer!"

"Devil!"

"Jesus loves you!"

"Slut!"

It should have been indecipherable, but the voices were so different, they each called for attention. The girls couldn't help it, they looked at the different faces.

Hate.

Concern.

Caring.

Anger.

Disgust.

They were all there. It was hard to look away. Finally, Mrs. A was able to open the door, and reached in to unlock the back door. She closed the doors after the girls got in. They immediately locked their doors, and Cate reached over to unlock the driver's door for Mrs. A.

Because Mrs. A had backed into the parking spot, she was able to pull away rather easily. The picketers reluctantly gave way and the three were on the street heading for home. The girls were quiet. Mrs. A paid attention to her driving and they soon arrived home.

There was no lunch out.

* * * * * * *

They took turns in the bathroom and met again in the kitchen. Mrs. A made lemonade, the frozen can kind. They pulled sandwich materials out and each made up a plate of food. "Take them outside?" Mrs. A offered, opening a bag of chips. She opened the Tupperware full of celery, carrots, broccoli and cauliflower that was always in the fridge.

They sat near the burned wall and ate in silence.

"That was sure fun," Cheryl began the conversation.

"Real fun," Cate added. "Do those people think they're really helping?"

"You know, they'll do anything." Cheryl was into it again. "I don't mean those people at the clinic. I mean those people in general. They think they know best. They think God is on their side. They think He gives them the right to do anything to stop us."

"At least we have the law on our side now," Cate responded. "They can't stop us. But not everyone is strong enough to stand up to that and come back the next day, or whenever the appointment is. Did you get an appointment?" Cate asked Cheryl.

Cheryl looked uncomfortable. "I'll take these dishes into the kitchen." She quickly stacked up their dishes and hurried into the house. Cate looked at Mrs. A. They both seemed puzzled. Cate got up and followed her new friend.

"What's the matter with you?" Cate asked Cheryl. "Did you get bad news?"

"None of your business!" Cheryl snapped.

"That's true," Cate was looking at her. Cheryl was leaning against the sink, her arms crossed tightly over her chest. She was looking at the floor. Her eyes were squeezed shut, but tears still ran down her cheek. She sniffed and swore.

"Damn! Damn it!"

Cate moved to her and put first one arm and then the other around the other girl's shoulders. "What is it? What happened?"

"It's too late!"

"What?" Cate was aghast.

"Too late! I waited too long! They won't do it. Well they will do it, but I won't. They would have to kill it, you know? Something about 'partial birth.' It's gruesome. I can't do it! I can't."

"Oh my God," Cate whispered. "Oh my God." They stood together. One girl sobbing in the arms of the other. "What are you going to do?"

The sobbing slowed and the girls started to separate. "I don't know. I can't kill it. And I certainly can't kill us." Her voice was rising, almost to the point of hysteria. "What will I do? What will I do?"

Mrs. A came through the door. She heard the desperate questions. She saw the two huddled together. She quickly approached them. They turned toward her and she took their hands and led them to the table. "It's time," she began. They all sat down. Silence fell on the table between them.

Cheryl wiped her nose and stifled the sobs and sniffles. The tears stopped flowing and she looked up at Mrs. A with deep sadness. "I'm too far along. I can't kill it."

"Then something has to change. You have to make a decision. Did the clinic representative give you any leads?" Mrs. A looked at her intensely. "That piece of paper in your pocket?"

"Oh, that. Well, she talked about adoption. That's probably the best idea."

"Did she tell you how to go about that?" The older woman was watching her closely. Cheryl seemed so tired. The energy was gone from her thin face. She looked defeated.

"No. I mean, I don't know. I think I went into shock. I couldn't hear her. She gave me the paper. I don't even remember walking out. The first thing I remember after is standing with Cate at the brochures. I grabbed the one on adoption." She dug in her pocket and brought out a couple of glossy brochures. "I know what they do at this stage. The baby could live, but they kill it before it comes out. Oh my God. Oh God," she moaned.

Cate was looking at her. "But you could still do it and go on with your life, like you planned."

"No. I couldn't. It could live."

"Are you going to call your mom and dad now?" Mrs. A asked. "They could really help you now. You'll need support."

"You mean I have to leave? Can't I stay here? I wouldn't be any trouble. I could help you around here. Please, can't I stay?"

"Of course you can stay. But I need to know it's all right with your parents. And you need a plan. And it looks like you need a nap. Why don't you head upstairs and rest. Clear your head. We'll work out a plan later. You've had quite a shock this morning."

"Thanks. I am tired. I'm worn out. I could sleep forever."

"No, not forever, Cheryl. I'll be up later. We'll start the arrangements."

..*.*.*.*

They watched her leave the kitchen and continued in silence for a few minutes. Cate put her head down on her arms on the table. Mrs. A reached over and stroked her hair.

"Grandma? That's awful. All her plans…."

"But you have to respect her decision."

"I do. But…. I don't know if she made the right choice. I mean, well, at least she isn't going to try to raise it like her mother wants her to."

"She's a strong girl, but with this turn of events, you know, she may change her mind again when she talks with her parents."

"But she seemed afraid for her dad to know. Does she have to tell them?"

"All the agencies will want to know about her background. And remember, we don't know how old she is. If she's a minor, her parents will have to know. I didn't bring that up before, but I'm sure they did at the clinic. I didn't want to influence her thinking by putting up roadblocks. But there are many more for her than for you. Speaking of you?"

"I made an appointment for the day after tomorrow. It's early, so hopefully there won't be too many creeps around the clinic."

"They're not 'creeps,' Cate. They're people with deep beliefs. Some of their actions are, well yes, 'creepy.' I'd say some of their actions are downright evil. But the police try to control their actions. To protect others' rights."

"I know that, Grandma, but they make it so hard."

"Don't you think it should be hard? Don't you think that we should think a lot about what we're doing?"

"There's not much for me to think about. None of this is my fault and I'm not going to pay for it for the rest of my life. I just want it all to go away, you know? Like nothing happened."

"But it did happen. It happened to you. You'll never forget it. Believe me. It'll pop up in your life when you least expect it. Even with no baby, no evidence of it, it will still be in your life. You'll need counseling. Your mom and I have talked about it. No matter what you do about the baby, we will take care of you. We will see that you get whatever you nccd."

"I'm not doing counseling. And I don't want to talk about it anymore. It was hard enough telling you two. When this is done, I'll just go on. It'll be like it was before. More or less."

"Yes, 'more or less.' We'll be here to help you… whatever happens."

"I know Grandma." A long silence stretched between them. They were comfortable with the quiet.

..*.*.*.*.*

Cheryl had asked for a couple days before she called home. She agreed to ask her mom to come over and meet Mrs. A, and they would work together to make the adoption happen. Cheryl said she would find out what she could about agencies, and hospitals. She also said she had arranged to see a doctor but thought she should talk with her mother first. She didn't want to cause too much trouble, until Cate had her appointment.

"Mrs. A," Cheryl's voice was almost a whisper. She had been hanging back since they had returned from the clinic. She was careful not to look up. She had been quiet, but then so had Cate. The clinic experience usually brought out all kinds of different behavior. Or so Mrs. A had noticed. Instead of angry and rebellious, these two were thoughtful and quiet. They were both isolated by their experiences. Cocooned in their thoughts. In spite of their laughter over the materials when they had picked them up, they devoured them silently now. Passed them back and forth without comment. There were pamphlets on contraception, prenatal care, a child's first year, legal rights, responsibilities, abortion, and fetal development. They were all in a pile on the dining room table now. Their information tromping through the readers' brains.

"How are you doing, Cheryl?"

"Not very good."

"Are you sick?"

"Oh no! I mean, I'm not going to throw up or anything. It's not that. I'm just kinda mixed up."

"Did you understand what they told you?"

"Yeh. Ah, well, most of it. It's so hard to…. They were really kind. When I started to cry, the doctor even held my hand." Tears were rolling now. And Mrs. A put her arms around the young girl who began to sob and hid her face in Mrs. A's shoulder.

They stood there together in the kitchen until the sobs stopped. Cheryl sagged onto a chair at the table and Mrs. A handed her the Kleenex box from the counter. She reached across for Cheryl's hands after she was done mopping her face and neck and blowing her nose. The piles of soggy Kleenex spotted the table around their hands.

"Can I help you, honey?"

"No, you've done so much already."

"Can you tell me about it?"

"No! It.... It's.... No, you'd hate me. You'd think I'm so stupid. It was supposed to be so simple. But everyone cares so much. You.... You've been so good to me. I don't want to ruin that."

"Nothing's going to ruin that, Cheryl. This is who we are. You need help and I help. It's so natural. We're human. We need help. We need to help." Mrs. A was patting Cheryl's hand and stroking her hair. Her soothing voice was almost a lullaby. Cheryl's sniffles were less and less frequent. Deep sighs took their place.

Finally, Mrs. A continued. "Would you like to call your mom?"

"No! Why would you say that? Not yet. Or my dad. I can handle this myself. I just need time to think. I just need to stay here."

"Did you make an appointment? Schedule anything at the clinic?"

"I can't talk about it yet. Please. Let me have some time. I'm so mixed up."

"I can see that. Do you think you could talk with Cate? You have so much in common."

"Not really, our stories are so different."

"Pregnancy is pregnancy, Cheryl. That story is not different. And you are so brave. Remember that first night? When everyone was here?"

"That was some other girl. I don't know how I did that."

"Well, you were really cornered. But very brave. Not that they aren't nice people."

"Yeh, I was very comfortable that night. And I still am. But still. Cate and I…. Well, I don't know what…. I mean, she made an appointment didn't she? I'm not sure that I…. Or that…. I'm just not sure." And she jumped up from the table and crashed through the kitchen door. She pounded up the stairs and slammed the bedroom door. Mrs. A knew the sobs continued even though she suspected they were smothered by a pillow.

She followed the teenager through the door and saw Cate staring angrily at her. "You shouldn't let her yell at you like that Grandma."

"She's not yelling at me, honey. She's just yelling. Probably because she can't find the words to tell me how she's feeling. Maybe she doesn't even know how she's feeling. How are you feeling? You've been pretty quiet since we got back."

"I wish I could feel differently about it, but I just have to do this. The other options just aren't right for me. God! That sounds selfish! Me! Me! Me!"

Mrs. A pulled out a dining room chair. The scraping sound broke the noisy silence after the "me, me, me." Cate plopped down on the floor.

"They certainly explained it all to me. And I listened like you said. They didn't ask me too many questions. But I almost laughed when they asked if I wanted the father involved. But I just said 'no.' They didn't make me feel bad. I mean, I already feel bad. But they didn't go on and on. They had things to say. And I listened. I didn't have very many questions, but I could have asked more. If I wanted. I did ask how they could do this job."

What did they say, honey?"

"They said all their services were helpful and needed by women. That a woman's body needed special care. That women had a right to have that care. Someone needs to provide that care. You know, Grandma? That's where Mom is wrong. Not everyone can do this. You know, what you do. Or the work the clinic does. But it's so important that the clinic does this work. Somebody has to be there. Somebody…."

"There always has been somebody. But every woman has to find her own way. For some it was easier than others. If you had money, your family doctor might do it. If he wouldn't, the women would tell each other and he would find himself with no business at all. In most families, women made the decisions about health care. But if you were poor, your options were harder. Dirtier. More dangerous. Even I couldn't take in those with the botched abortions. I just took them to the hospital. Sometimes I cared for them after. The doctors or the police would tell them about me. But if I hadn't taken them to the hospital and they died on me, then I would have been blamed and then I would have been able to help no one. One mother accused me of killing her daughter. I had only taken her to the hospital. But the daughter stayed alive long enough to say I didn't do it, and my hospital friends spoke up for me. But that was a scary time. I don't know why I even thought about it now."

"Things are better now, Grandma, right?"

"Well, I suppose we could say there doesn't have to be any unwanted pregnancies, but I think there always will be. Science can help, but we're still humans. Look at your own story. Sometimes, we can't control what happens to us."

"Or we don't want to."

"You're right of course," Mrs. A sighed. "Anyway, what did you set up this morning or did you?"

"Yes," Cate glanced away. "Yes, Thursday morning. Ten a.m. Unless there's a cancellation. I'm supposed to be there about eight, no eating or drinking after midnight. I'm so tired Grandma."

"Why don't you go on upstairs and rest. Sounds like Cheryl's cried herself out. She's probably asleep or almost."

"I guess I will." She headed up the stairs slowly, sadly.

..*.*.*.*.*

Cheryl was alone upstairs. She thought she had better call her mother and tell her about the clinic. She closed the door to the office and dialed the phone.

"Hi, Mom. Yes, I'm alone. I know, I saw him there. No, I didn't say anything. Do you think I want them to know that my own dad is a picketer? I told Mrs. A it was too late. Well, they examined me and said I wasn't pregnant. I just kept telling them that I was sure I was. They said something like 'hysteria.' Yeh, 'hysterical pregnancy.' That's it. Well, they gave me a prescription for the pill. Mrs. A wants to meet with you about adoption. No, not right away. Cate's got an appointment and I said I would wait until after. What else can I do? She's not listening to anyone. Not even her mother. Don't call her that, Mom. She's really sweet and this isn't her fault. And Mrs. A is super nice. I know you didn't send me here to 'fall in love' with her. But she's really nice. I like her. She doesn't push. In fact, she doesn't say much at all about what to do. She makes us do all the work. She's letting me stay for now. Did you guys put nails on the driveway? No? Really? I thought OSB did it. That's funny, Cate's mom had three flat tires the other night. Yeh, nails. Well, maybe there's another group after Mrs. A. What do you want me to do next? Okay. I'll just keep watching. You know about the Molotov cocktail, right? The fire chief says it was an inside job. I know. You said you guys had nothing to do with it. No, she just sat with us in the reception room. Then she drove us back here. Okay. I love you too. Tell Daddy I love him. But he really looked scary at the clinic today. I know it's important work. But I really hate all this lying. Okay. Bye now." She put the receiver down and stared at the floor. The sun was going in and out of the clouds. It brought light and dark to the room.

She felt light and dark too, one minute sure of what she was doing and the next hating spying on Mrs. A. She heard rattling pans from the kitchen and thought she would go help with dinner.

Chapter 13

Cate and her mom had had many loud talks about the plans, but Cate was unbending. Finally, there was a truce. Mia seemed resigned, but unhappy. She hung around, but would talk to no one.

"Mom, why don't you go home. I'm not going to change my mind. And you're not going with me. So, give it up. Go home, please. You're only making things harder."

"Evidently not hard enough. I know, I know. You've made up your mind. And I suppose I have to get over it. But, honey, you just don't understand…."

"Mom, I've been over and over it. This is what I have to do. I wouldn't try to change your mind and I think you should respect my decision. I'll call you when it's done, if you want me to."

"Oh God, Cate, of course I want you to call. You know I would be there if you would let me." They held each other for a long while. "You better get to bed. Do you think you can sleep? Maybe I should stay."

"I'll be okay, Mom. I'm really tired. It's been tough around here. But I'm fine. In fact, I'm really good. This is right for me. This is what I need to do. You go home. Sleep in your own bed. I'll be okay."

"Can I call you before…?"

"No! No. Don't call. I think I'd rather not, you know. I do love you, Mom. Now go. Go home."

After the door closed, Cate covered her face and bent over at the waist. Her hands moved down to her belly and caressed the swelling. She straightened up with her hands supporting the bulge that was beginning to show big time. She felt the little flutter. She shook her head no. It was only gas. She went up the stairs to bed.

..*.*.*.*.*

Cate didn't know it would hurt so much. She thought she was prepared. They were standing around her at the foot of the table. They had talked with her. Explained everything again. She knew what they were going to do. They had draped her. Had inserted the I.V. Her grandma was there. She thought it would be easier. She heard them talking. Chatting for God's sake! "Ready?" they said not waiting for an answer. "Sure." She thought she could take the pain. She reached out her hand to her grandma and she was right there, stepping right up, taking Cate's hand firmly in both of her warm, dry, wrinkled chicken feet hands.

The cold speculum was inside her. The pain brought up terrifying memories. She began to sweat. She wanted to cover her eyes, but they had her "mummy wrapped" and she couldn't move her arms. She closed her eyes as tight as she could, but the memories were more vivid then. She stared at the lights above her. She was so confused. She wanted to be brave. She looked at her grandma's face. She found some peace there and hung onto that peace until she heard the vacuum. "Am I right, Grandma?" she whispered. And she felt the dull pull in her uterus. She was empty. It was gone. She didn't want to moan. Or cry. Or faint.

..*.*.*.*.*

Mrs. A sighed. Here she was again. Standing by. She couldn't count how many women had needed her. But it was so much better now. The law was there. Roe v. Wade was decided and already the procedure was safer. After care was more reliable. Clinics and hospitals provided clean, consistent care. Knowledge and science enabled secure preventive measures. Now there was something a woman could actually count on, rather than getting "caught." But….

Mrs. A heard the clinic staff chatting as they stood at the foot of the table. They were good people doing their job. But she knew them and she knew that the job was hard on them. They believed in the work. They were professionals. But she knew the agony they hid. She had worked with them for a long time. She had coffee with them. She cried with them.

She looked toward the woman on the table. Her granddaughter, Cate. Her feet in the stirrups, her legs tented. The rest of her body lay on the other side of the barrier, separately draped. They were ready to begin. The doctor reached out and spread her knees. The nurse asked "Ready?"

Cate reached out to her. Mrs. A stepped closer. Covered her granddaughter's hand with both of her own. Willing her strength to flow through the connection.

The bright lights fractured the room. She concentrated on the girl on the table. But she couldn't prevent the thoughts of the fractured lives of the other women and girls she had helped.

Cate was squeezing her hand. Hard. She was whimpering. Mrs. A put one hand on her shoulder and the whimper changed to a moan. They were looking at each other. Mrs. A reached up to brush her granddaughter's hair out of her eyes and pet her gently. Tears were coming now. "Am I right, Grandma?" It was just a whisper. The sob was very soft too. Really, a choked off sigh. And then she fainted.

The nurse looked up and checked her patient's pulse. She rolled one of Cate's eyelids back and consoled Mrs. A. "She's fine. It happens sometimes. Probably from the stress. But then why am I telling you?" She smiled. They had worked together many times. "She'll be all right. We're almost done."

..*.*.*.*.*

They had moved down the hall to the recovery room. The nurses were checking Cate's pads and vitals regularly. And soon they would release her. Mrs. A was sitting next to the bed. Her granddaughter stirred and tried to sit up.

"Whoa! You're supposed to lie still until the nurse okays anything else. You don't want to bring on excessive bleeding. It doesn't take long, but it is necessary."

"Did they say anything? Was it…normal?"

"They don't usually discuss the fetus, honey. They are here to take care of you."

"What do they do with it? Can I see it?"

"I don't think…." Mrs. A stopped. Maybe Cate needed to see it. "Why would you want to see it?"

"Don't know. Probably not a good idea anyway. But do you think you could tell the color, or something…. You know…. About the man who….?"

The nurse came into the room just then. "Mrs. A, there's somebody in the lobby. I guess she has something for you."

"Okay," Mrs. A said. "Cate has some questions. Could you help her? I'll be right back, Hon. Just take your time. Okay?"

"Okay."

And Mrs. A was out the door, walking down the hall.

..*.*.*.*.*

Cheryl heard the front door open. Mrs. A and Cate had just left for the clinic. "Did you forget something?" she called as she came from the kitchen. Mia was standing in the front hall holding a backpack.

"Cate called and said she had forgotten her backpack. I drove over here to get it, but…. You know, she didn't want me there. Maybe you can help. If I drive you over, you could run it in for her. Then she wouldn't see me and get upset. I don't want to upset her today. Would you do that?"

"Sure, just a minute. I'll clear up my mess in the kitchen."

"Thanks, Cheryl. I'll wait out in the car." She watched the young girl go into the kitchen. A sly smile crossed over her face. She squared her shoulders and hefted the backpack. With a clatter and a sound of running water coming from the kitchen, she went out the front door, striding triumphantly down the walk to her car.

Cheryl slammed the door behind her and ran down the walk to the car. "I don't know why she needs the backpack, she'll be home this afternoon already. I suppose she thinks she can read before and after. I don't think I could concentrate enough."

"I don't know, I'm just doing what she asked. I'm very glad you can help though. How are you feeling?"

They drove the route to the clinic, cheerily chatting like casual acquaintances. The older woman asked a lot about school and friends, schoolwork, and activities. They arrived quickly and Mia pulled the car up to the front. The picketers quickly moved toward the car. Cheryl grabbed the backpack from the floor. "Oof! What is she reading, the encyclopedia?"

Mia laughed. "You girls. You need to have everything you own with you, just in case."

Cheryl jumped out of the car and ran into the clinic, dashing past the picketers who started their routine in order to stop her. Once she was inside, Mia started to dig in her purse and pulled out a small box with a button. It looked like a garage opener. She held the box in one hand, while she looked at her watch. She could see Cheryl through the glass door. She was talking with the receptionist. She glanced at the protesters and hoped they wouldn't get in her way. But they were watching Cheryl too.

Inside, the receptionist looked up. "Welcome back. You're Cheryl, right? You came in with Mrs. A the other day. Sure. But do you have an appointment today?" She seemed a little puzzled.

"No, I'm here to bring Cate her backpack."

"Oh, she's not available now. They got started early. There was a cancellation. But I can take it in and put it in her locker, or give it to Mrs. A." She reached for the phone and pushed a button. "Someone brought a backpack for Cate Mayer. Do you want to come get it, or should Mrs. A? Okay." She hung up the phone. "I'll meet you at the door over there, Cheryl," she said and disappeared through a door and reappeared at the other door that led to the exam rooms. Cheryl walked over and started to hand the backpack to the receptionist. She saw Mrs. A coming down the hall.

"Hi, Mrs. A," she called to the older woman.

..*.*.*.*.*

The response was lost in the explosion. Cheryl and the receptionist disappeared in a bloody vapor and metal shower that flew out from between them. Their bodies thudded to the floor yards away from each other. Mrs. A was forced back down the hall and landed on her back with the blood, metal and wood entering her body, face and arms. Her own blood soon joined in covering her. She could feel her leg folded weirdly to the side. Everything was muffled. She couldn't hear and with the blood in her eyes, she couldn't see. Someone ran past. Someone else was kneeling next to her. She could see that person yelling at her, but she couldn't hear or answer. They were joined by a third woman who took one look at her and rushed off.

The first woman stayed with her. She kept talking, sometimes to her and sometimes to other people rushing around. She felt the pounding of running feet and rolled her head slightly to see who was coming. Two of the pounding feet belonged to her daughter. She appeared briefly and mouthed "I'm here, Mom." Mia grabbed her hand and Mrs. A tried to smile. That effort was enough for her to lose it and fade away.

**.*.*.*.*.*

After the ambulance left with her mother safely inside and the receptionist and Cheryl had been covered, waiting for whatever needed to be done. After the fire department left and the police had taken up their positions inside and out. After some semblance of order had been attained, they let her in to see her daughter.

Cate was glad to see her. She started sobbing as soon as she saw her mother. She raised her arms and Mia rushed into them. They held each other and cried.

"I had to do it, Mom. I'm sorry. I didn't want to be cruel to you, but I had to do it. And being around you, knowing how you feel about it, just made it so much harder."

"It's over now. We can't undo it, but we can stop it from undoing us." As they held each other, she overheard the nurses in the hallway.

"Oh my God!"

"Can you believe it?"

"No! How did she fool Shelly?"

"Lord, I don't know. All the policies, the training.... This isn't supposed to happen."

"It's supposed to be impossible."

"I guess nothing is impossible."

"But who would've thought. Wasn't she here the other day?"

"Yeh, with Mrs. A."

"So, how...?"

"She wasn't pregnant. Dr. Johnson gave her a prescription for the pill."

"Not pregnant?"

"No, she said she was, but no. Johnson said something about 'hysteria.'"

"Well, we've had a few like that before, but...."

"Yeh...."

And they were gone. Mia was sitting with Cate in the recovery room. She hadn't known about the cancellation. She was too late to save her grandbaby, but she was sure the rest of the plan would work. And Cheryl wasn't even pregnant. She had them all fooled. What was with her anyway? Why was she at her mom's? If she wasn't pregnant. "Hysterical pregnancies." Plenty of couples got married because of that. You could be fooled. Was Cheryl fooled? Or.... Anyway, it was useful to her cause. She was home free. No one would suspect.

Cate was stirring. Her left hand was reaching for her belly. She moaned softly. Mia moved the hand away from the belly and held it in her own two hands. She spoke softly to her daughter, almost crooning. "I love you, sweetheart. I'll take care of you and Grandma too."

Chapter 14

Mrs. A awoke in the hospital again. They were standing at the bottom of the bed looking at a chart and at her. They were talking in whispers, not chatting, but something about a "bomb" and a "clinic." She was naked under the drape. They had inserted an I.V. How could she take the pain? She didn't want to moan. Or cause trouble. Gradually, she could feel the effect of the I.V and she gave herself up to it.

After they were done removing the foreign objects from her flesh she awoke to see the nurse standing next to the bed. "Well, you finally decided to rejoin us. I told you it would hurt. You took the easy way out. But I don't blame you. You did fine. The doctor is satisfied that he got all of that junk out. You're lucky. Well, I guess it's all relative. I guess there was quite a mess over there. They said people were cheering, you know, the picketers outside. But maybe you don't know what happened. Your daughter is here, she'll fill you in. She's been waiting outside. Got here right away after they brought you in. I'll get her for you." And she was gone.

..*.*.*.*.*

Mrs. A had shut her eyes again…just for a moment. Mia peeked around the door and thought she was sleeping. She walked quietly to the chair next to the bed. Once again, she looked through the railing at her mother. This time it was worse. One eye was covered with a big piece of cotton held on with that hospital tape. Her hair was caked with blood. Small bandages stepped up her arms. Other cuts were big enough for stitches. One leg was in a cast.

Mia sat and waited patiently until her mother woke again. It wasn't long and her eye flickered and opened to reveal confusion and distress. Mrs. A gurgled a little as she asked, "Cate?"

"She's okay. They let me see her. She was in recovery, but she was okay. They said they started her procedure early. Evidently there was a cancellation. I didn't know that. But she's safe. The bomb didn't hurt her. I have to go soon to pick her up. She had to give permission for me to see her. And she had to sign something to let me take her home. But it'll all work out."

"Bomb?"

"Yeh. In fact, I'm an accessory. I have to talk with the police. But not today. Today I have to take care of Cate and you. So, they're going to wait."

"You?"

"Not really. Unknowing."

"Cheryl?"

"Didn't make it. Neither did the receptionist. What a tragedy! Why would she do that?"

"Do what?"

"The bomb. She brought in the bomb."

"No," Mrs. A sobbed. "No, she wouldn't."

"They say she did. It must have been in the backpack. She called me and said Cate had forgotten her backpack and asked me to help get it to her."

"No," came the soft denial from Mrs. A. "No."

"They said she wasn't pregnant. They had given her a prescription for birth control pills and counseling on preventing venereal disease. They said she didn't seem surprised. I think you were set up, Mom. I think they finally got to you."

"The fire?"

"Yeh, that was probably her too. It had to be one of the four of us. Cheryl was the only real suspect, I don't care what the Chief insinuated. Was Cheryl even her real name? What did you know about her?"

Mrs. A moaned and closed her eye. "I'm sorry, Mom. You sleep. You can come home with me soon. I'll take care of you. You don't have to go on with that life anymore. The 'girls' will have to find another helper."

Mia leaned down and kissed her sleeping mother on the forehead. A triumphant smile took over her face. For a moment she stood there, patting her mother, stroking her hair. Then she gathered her things and with a sober face, left the room to go and get her daughter and take her home.

BIOGRAPHY

Marj Helmer

Helmer has been a student, high school German teacher, mom, feminist, volunteer, office worker, business owner, political candidatc, grandma, and all-round cheerleader. Currently she is a writer with rejchapections to prove it! She writes fiction based on life issues. This novel, **Mrs. A's Tea Party** is about abortion and three generations of women dealing with unwanted pregnancies. Her second novel. **Coffee With Mrs. A,** continues the story of Cate and her work for women. Helmer covers "end-of-life" issues at **the Abide-A-While Resort**. Helmer is the editor of **the Maple Grove Writers' Studio Anthology Bits and Pieces 1 and 2**. She believes in the individual, and in learning as a life-long obligation. She lives in Maple Grove,

Minnesota. Contact her at mhelmer.author@gmail.com. Contact the Maple Grove Writers' Studio at maplegrovewritersstudio@gmail.com

Coming soon from Amazon!

Coffee With Mrs. A

The Women March Onward

Sequel to ***Mrs. A's Tea Party***

By Marj Helme

Chapter 1

Mrs. A was recuperating at her daughter's. Mia had brought her home from the hospital after the bombing at the clinic and was happily caring for her with the help of her daughter Cate.

Cate had escaped injury. She had been in one of the treatment rooms finishing her abortion when the bomb exploded. They had heard the explosion even in there. In shock, the clinic staff locked the door and sealed it with towels to prevent smoke from coming in. That was the policy. The doctor continued with the D and C that would relieve Cate of the product of rape. That was also the policy.

Mrs. A's injuries were severe. A broken leg, one eye lost, a concussion causing severe headaches with tears and nausea. It was impossible to recognize her with the many deep cuts and bruises. She slept a lot. Cate sat with her during the day, while her mother worked at the bank. Jimmy, Cate's brother was also helping, if reluctantly. He hated being inside, and after school, he played football and just generally hung around with his friends.

Cate hadn't returned to school yet. She was supposed to start at the University but had postponed everything. She had recovered from her abortion fine, but the shock of the bombing of the clinic and the deaths of her friend, Cheryl, and the receptionist, overwhelmed them all. It was in the papers and on the radio and television. They couldn't hide from it, but they were in hiding. They left the phone off the hook and they peeked out the living room window, to see who was at the door. They only answered when it was someone they knew.

Those people were their friends and family who had flocked to their aid. Hotdishes filled the freezer. Delicious tuna, goulash, hamburger, turkey, and veggie hotdishes. To stick in a preheated 375 degree oven for a half hour, serve and eat. The visits had to be brief because of the headaches, concussion, and weakness due to blood loss that stymied Mrs. A.. But she was happy to see them, and grateful for the support. She was surprised how many of her "girls" stopped by. They were mostly shy and quietly sat next to her bed. Most said very little. Some wept or cried as they looked at her with her swollen face and other wounds.

Coming soon from Amazon!

Abide-A-While Resort

How Do I End My Life?

A Novel

By Marj Helmer

George has a great idea. He will buy the resort his family use to go to and make it into a ...Wha? A kind of hospice? An elder resort? A care center? An end-of-life respite place? Yeh! All of the above

Five rugged cabins with screened porches, nestled around a couple of picnic tables and a bunch of Adirondack chairs in a green grassy area with a barbecue and a fire pit. Yeh! The combo rec room/office would do as the resort center like it had when he was a kid. He wondered if the swings, slide, sandbox, and shuffleboard court were still there. He's heard that it was for sale. A great summer get-a-way place! A great place to die?

Made in the USA
Monee, IL
23 August 2022

11323349R00105